# *Ratchet to Righteous 2*

This story is completely fictional. Any similarities to any people and events are completely coincidental. While there may be mention of known celebrities, places, or songs, all events are made up and in not any way related to actual events.

# Acknowledgements

I would first like to thank all my supporters who have helped to make this dream a reality. It still seems so surreal to have someone come up to me and compliment me on my writing. So, I not only thank you for your support, but the reviews and comments that has made me confident about the work I've put forth.

I continue to thank my husband Keith and my children Kyla and Jaxon for tolerating any slack on my part due to trying to multitask while taking care of home and producing quality writing. And thank you for your faith in me and your undying support.

Thank you to my mother LaVoe Sr., and my dad Duane for supporting me and making every event a success. As well as their contribution to the person I have become.

X Blu Rayne you are the best! You seem to know what I'm thinking without me having to say a word. Thanks to you, the dopest designer.

Bianca, Gabrielle, and Viva thank you for promoting and for the influence you all had in making this series a success.

And Wanakee, thank you again for being there from the beginning and keeping me on track. Good luck on your writing endeavors!

Finally, to my Heavenly Father, thank you for all the gifts you have bestowed upon me and the opportunity to allow me to use them to do your work. I pray for continued success.

## Dedications

I dedicate this book to my father, James Laney and my friend, Monet Campbell. I know you're both smiling down on me from Heaven.
A Special dedication to my grandmother, LaVeau "Moms" Amick.
Even from the stars you remain the matriarch of this family.

# Chapters

Ratchet- adj.
1. The astronomical levels of HOEING and the displaying on extreme levels, of GHETTO.

2. One who is very random and acts in ways of being LOUD & OBNOXIOUS

3. One who is DIRTY, LOW CLASS, NO MORAL VALVES and place themselves in a situation of
being known in NEGATIVE WAY.

4. The JEALOUS, LONELY & BUSTA of the group


Righteous- adj.
1. Morally upright; without guilt or sin: a righteous parishioner.

2. In accordance with virtue or morality: a righteous judgment.

3. Morally justifiable: righteous anger

*Sapphire*
*{Six years ago}*

It was the end of the summer and New York City seemed to be on fire. Red had just started school at NYC and was attempting to stay focused on her studies. But with her sister Peaches in town from St. Louis, it was almost impossible. Peaches was two years older than Red, but was nowhere near as responsible as her younger sister.

"So, you really finna study on a Friday night?" Peaches asked Red while she stood in the full-length mirror in Red's dorm room getting dressed for the night ahead.

She got a job at the Sapphire Gentlemen's Club when she visited this past summer, and tonight she was trying to convince Red to go with her.

"It's a gentlemen's club Peach. Do I look like a gentleman to you? Besides, I gotta study. I'm not starting school irresponsibly messing around with you." Red said as she buried her head back into her communications book.

"Yo borin' ass is gone waste away in them damn books. Me, I'm 'bout to get this money from Big John." Peaches said turning her back to the mirror and making her butt cheeks clap together.

9

*"Whatever heffa." Red said shaking her head at Peaches' actions. "You*
*betta learn how to get this money from these white mutha fuckas, especially since you finna be out here by yourself" Peaches said looking at Red who had a pencil behind her ear. "And he got entertainment connects, but he scared to hook me up though, he think I'm a dip on dat ass. He betta be." Peaches laughed at her own comment as she admired the way her body looked in her hot pink, see through cat suit.*

*Red barely heard her rambling through her own studying. "Yeah, yeah. Have fun for both of us." Red waved Peaches off.*

That was six years ago, and that conversation has played over and over in Red's mind. Over the past month, she had desperately tried to find out how her now physically and mentally disabled big sister Peaches, managed to have two children by Red's now deceased, married boyfriend. 'Big John,' could've definitely been short for Jonathan and the mention of the entertainment industry all struck a nerve.

Jonathan Grant was the CEO of Affinity Entertainment and Red's former 'sponsor'. After finding out that her sister had two children by Mr. Grant without even knowing they were acquainted in any way, she had been trying to jog her memory of any mention of him from Peaches in the past. When she recalled that day, she realized Peaches had been keeping this to herself for the two years that she'd dated him. Even longer really, considering Red's niece and nephew were now four and five years old.

It was the middle of the night as her mind turned in a million directions. She walked down the hall to check on Raina and Ryan at the thought of them. They were sound asleep. After the attempted murder on her life, Peaches had around the clock nursing care, so Red didn't feel any need to bother the staff watching after her. Not to mention the fact that she was still feeling resentment toward Peaches for the roller coaster ride she had been on for the past year.

First, Mr. Grant had a heart attack and died. Then she gets pregnant by her new boyfriend, who tried to kill her sister and now she doesn't know if he's dead or alive.

Red rubbed her perfectly round belly as she made it back to the master bedroom. She was nine months pregnant, thirty-nine weeks to be exact, and was due any day now. Thoughts of her baby's father Romero, made her think about the newly found relationship she had begun to redevelop with her childhood friend Toni. Toni just happened to be Romero's ex-lover and the reason Romero tried to murder her sister. But as complicated as it all was in her mind; her heart had actually come to like the person Toni had become.

Before, Red couldn't stand to be around her for more than a few minutes, unless it pertained to business. Toni's arrogance was a lot to deal with on a regular basis. But now, Red noticed how beautiful she actually was because it illuminated from the inside of her. Toni was a completely different person.

Red picked up the TV remote and turned the television to TRUtv.
The Dumbest Ever was on so she climbed into her king-sized canopy bed to try to get comfortable. She tossed and turned all night because neither her mind nor her body would let her rest. Just as she got snug directly in the center of the bed, GUSH!

"Oh shit, my water broke!"

A Dying Breed


"I can't remember the first time I felt this sexual." She thought as she looked at herself in the mirror. She had to be about three or four years old the first time her emergency babysitter Robert touched her.

Quitta was a sixteen-year-old that was a virgin by definition. But she had been touched sexually by numerous pedophiles and peers over her young life. She was considered easy by her peers because she had no qualms offering oral sexual favors to the boys in her neighborhood. Having no siblings made it easy for Quitta to get away with more than she probably would have; otherwise without anyone to witness her wrong doings, or the wrong that had been done to her. Either way she never protested.

Her mother Gwen was an excellent provider. She worked a corporate job with good benefits. She actually had a career and she made sure Quitta had the best of everything. However, with all the material things she received, Quitta never felt loved or wanted by anyone, including Gwen. Gwen never had time for anything but herself, and her father Franklin didn't help much with her self-esteem either. He was absent financially and emotionally. To her, her cat Shadow was her closest family member.

The relationship between her mother and father ended so badly, that Franklin refused to deal with Gwen in any shape, form, or fashion, including when it came to his daughter. In fact, he had a new wife and two other children that he took care of like royalty. But none of that mattered to Quitta, at least not on the surface.

She always found a way to make herself feel important, no matter how unhealthy or unsavory that way might have been. She smoked marijuana, drank alcohol, and popped ecstasy pills on a regular basis. Looking closer to twenty-six than sixteen allowed her to get the things she wanted with ease.

LaQuitta Renee Benton was about five-foot four with a bright yellow, but flawless complexion. She was top heavy, which made her appear slightly chubby, but she had legs like a model for a stockings ad. Her face was round like her light brown eyes and she had full pink lips. She also wore weave on a regularly, so her hair changed with her mood and this week it was long, black, and straight.

Today was special though, her school's head counselor, Mrs. Cameron, gave her a flyer to a youth program at her church. She always uplifted Quitta and told her how much potential she possessed. Mrs. Cameron was actually her favorite staff member at Jennings High School. She made Quitta feel like she genuinely cared about her. And although Mrs. Cameron was young, she was very intelligent in Quitta's eyes. She figured she must be, to be the head counselor of the entire district.

"Momma, I'm about to leave!" Quitta yelled through the house to her mother.

"Where are you going?" Gwen asked.

Gwen was getting dressed for an endeavor of her own. She was always looking for her next 'sponsor'.

"To church, it's right down the street!" Quitta yelled.

"Yeah okay." Gwen didn't believe her, but she didn't have time to be concerned, she had a date.

And normally she would've been right, but today was different, Quitta was actually excited about the program. Regardless to how physically advanced she was, her spirit yearned for something, anything.

As Quitta entered the church, the first person she noticed was Rocky. Rocky was her friend that went to school with her and was a self-proclaimed 'stud'. Quitta thought she was one of the prettiest girls she'd ever met, but it was hard to tell through the khakis and oversized tee shirts she wore most of the time. She had light caramel skin with hazel eyes. Her hair was long and naturally curly, but she kept it corn rolled and usually underneath some type of head gear. Rocky didn't want to accidentally be mistaken for a girl.

"Whatchu doin' here?" Quitta asked Rocky as she approached her.

"Mrs. Cameron gave me a flyer." Rocky held up the colorful piece of paper.

"Yeah, me too. I was hoping I would see somebody I know." Quitta said.

Quitta looked around the sanctuary at the banners and decoration

14

representing the spring festival at the church. She admired the art and creativity put into the decor. She was an artist in her own right, so arts and crafts always interested her.

"Hello ladies, I'm glad you both could make it." The girls heard the voice of their counselor approaching them from behind.

"Hi Mrs. Cameron." The two girls said in unison.

"We're not at school now, you can call me Ivey. That's what the other teens here call me." Ivey told them.

Quitta's heart almost stopped at the sight of a tall handsome man walking in their direction. All she saw was tall, dark, and handsome.

"Let me introduce you girls to my husband, Brandon. Brandon, this is LaQuitta and Raquel.

Quitta's heart broke. "Damn!" She thought as she extended her hand to greet the heart throb. She took every inch of him in. He was clean cut and shaven, and she thought the dimple in his chin was the sexiest thing she had ever seen. And his deep brown skin was as flawless as his smile.

Ivey pointed the girls in the direction of some empty seats, but Quitta wasn't snapped out of her gaze until Rocky elbowed her in the ribs.

"Bitch." Rocky whispered. "Can you be any more obvious? Close your mouth. Ew, you're disgusting, drooling over that woman's husband." Rocky said with her nose turned up at Quitta.

They approached the empty bench and took their seats.

"Anyway, Mrs. Cameron's fine ass gone be mine soon enough, then you can make your move." Rocky told Quitta with a straight face she could only hold for a few seconds before erupting into laughter.

Quitta joined in on the fun but to her this was no joke; her young mind was clouded by seduction and she had to find a way to get close to Brandon. Although Ivey was one of her favorite people, it didn't stop her from delving into the abyss of sexual conquest, no matter who she hurt in the process.

For the Love of Money


As Gwen pulled into the parking lot at the Resident's Inn in Westport, she took one last look at her makeup and applied a tad more Mac lip gloss. She was an older, slightly darker version of her daughter LaQuitta. The cleavage she toted on her E sized breast left nothing to the imagination.

She was meeting Clarence King. He was an executive at an Ad agency that she met through an online website for Sugar Daddies. They had been involved for about a month. Other than his job, his Jaguar, and how good he was in bed, she didn't know much more about him, nor did she care. He claimed to not be married, but she knew their time spent at hotels was not for a change of scenery. Past incidents with her daughter caused Gwen not to bring men back to her home, so if it stopped him from coming to her house. Hotels were okay with her.

When she exited her Jetta, Gwen made sure to check her reflection. She wore tight, dark blue, skinny leg jeans and a tan blazer with her tan pumps. Then she readjusted her cleavage to reveal even more skin in her black lace camisole.
Clarence opened the room door and instantly began to salivate.

"Damn sexy, did you bring a babysitter for those kids?" He said looking like he wanted to bury his face in her cleavage.

"Why, do they need a sitter? You need some help?" She asked as her mind quickly wandered to several men that she knew would be up for the task.

"I don't need help with what belongs to me." Clarence said looking at Gwen trying to gage her reaction.

"Yours? Now let's not get confused about what this is. You don't think I'm disillusioned into believing that you don't belong to someone already, do you?" The look she gave him was a reminder that her forty years did not make her a dummy.

"Whatchu talking about? This all you." He said pointing to himself
like she had won a prize.

She had to admit though, to be fifty Clarence was a handsome specimen. He worked out regularly and his body showed it. He was dark skinned, six foot three, and had mingly gray hair that he kept cut low along with his mingly gray goatee. *I just know he belongs to someone,* she thought as he stood there in his black Levis and white oxford.

"I like to play Clarence, just not with my intelligence. So, let's not go there today. What you got for me?" Gwen looked past him at the gift bag on the bed.

"Oh that?" He turned to look at the bag. "That's for my woman." He said facetiously.

"Whatever." She said as she tried to walk around him to get to the gift.

Just as she got beside him, he grabbed her arm, firmly but without
hurting her.

"You are my woman, right?" He asked, looking into her eyes with intensity.

"I'm whatever you want me to be." She said deciding she would go along with his story if it meant he would lighten up.

When he let her go she proceeded to the bed to see what gift the bag held. Inside the bag was a red Victoria's Secret lingerie ensemble and five crisp one hundred-dollar bills. He always came through with decent gifts and she loved the attention. But what she couldn't ignore was the roughness in his touch.

"So, are you always that rough with your 'woman'?" Gwen asked
giving air quotes with her question.

"No and I apologize if I made you uncomfortable. From now on, I'll be as gentle as a lamb." He told her with the sincerity of a promise.

Then he walked up to her and kissed her gently as if to prove what he was saying was the truth. He held her face and kissed her with passion then proceeded behind her. As he removed the blazer from her shoulders and back, he replaced every inch with a kiss. Her body began to react as she reached behind her to massage his well-endowed manhood.

"You smell so good." He whispered in her ear.

"You feel so good." She moaned referring to the pulsation that
commenced between her fingers. "Now let me see how you taste."

She turned to face him still holding his hardness. He eagerly anticipated what was to come and he hoped it was him. Gwen had a fetish, an oral fixation really. If Clarence knew how much she loved giving oral pleasure, he would've released where he stood. But she managed to contain her excitement, so no one would truly know how obsessed she really was. She had to swallow the excess saliva forming at the thought of the feeling of him in her mouth.

She dropped to her knees and took every inch of him down her throat until she gagged. A flood of juices filled her black lace bikini panties as she slurped and moaned until Clarence couldn't take another second.

"Aaaaauuuugh!" He screamed while releasing his seed onto Gwen's
full round breast.

She rubbed the semen across her chest like lotion with her eyes closed while she moaned the entire time. Clarence had never experienced a woman that loved to please a man the way she did. But what he didn't know is that she had a problem, Gwen was an addict.

It wasn't until she walked in on her ex-boyfriend Trey, who was fifteen years her junior, and her daughter Quitta. It was then that she realized that the apple didn't fall far from the tree.

"She won't suck this dick." She thought as she considered Quitta more as competition than as a daughter.

When it came to men, Gwen was relentless, and she trusted no woman.

Neither blood nor bond had been able to penetrate her love for men and money. Even when it came to her own flesh and blood, and whether he was worth it or not.

## Mercy

Toni sat in the Labor and Delivery waiting room at St. John's Mercy Hospital. The last time she was there, no one but God knew whether or not she would make it out alive, but here she was. Only this time she was there because she received an emergency phone call from Red telling her that she had gone into labor.

The irony was, around this time last year Toni and Red were in Atlanta having a knockdown, drag out fight at Romero's house. Now she was here supporting Red in her time of need. Her life had changed so much in the last year that it was even hard for her to believe at times.

Last year, she had been sleeping with Romero's best friend Jojo, which happened to be Peaches' alleged babies' daddy at the time. This caused a chain of events that started with Peaches plotting with Coco, someone else Toni had crossed in the past, to have Toni raped, beaten, and left for dead.

Before, she was a materialistic, manipulative, promiscuous, self-absorbed, gold digger. And she was at the point in her life where she could actually admit who she used to be in an effort to never return to that place again.

She felt there was a bond forming between her and Red. So, she felt a sense of camaraderie when Red called her when she went into labor, she was honored. Even though Toni felt some responsibility that Red was going through her pregnancy alone, she still felt privileged to be the first person that she contacted.

"Ms. Danes?" A petite blonde nurse said as she approached Toni.

"Yes." Toni said.

"We have Ms. Mason situated now, you can come back." The nurse led Toni to Red's room.

When Toni entered the room, Red looked exhausted. Her sew in was in complete disarray and she seemed exasperated.

"Hey lady, how are you feeling?" Toni asked as a courtesy, because it was clear from her looks how she felt.

"I'm better now that they gave me this epidural. Girl, I thought I was about to die." Red said with utter relief that her current contraction only felt like pressure compared to the last six hours of her labor.

"Well, I'm glad you called. Is everything alright with the baby?" Toni asked with concern.

"He's fine. They're just concerned about whether my pelvis will allow him to pass; they predict he will weigh almost ten pounds. So, they're making preparations in case they need to do an emergency C-section." Red sounded less than enthused.

"Well I'll be here as long as you need me, okay? Oh, do you need me to check on the kids?" Toni said as she smiled with sincerity and then found a place to get comfortable.

"No, they actually have a nanny and thank you Toni. I know we've had a rocky past, but I've noticed the difference in you and it's beautiful. I bet it's got something to do with that fine ass minister of yours." Red laughed as she shifted to endure the pressure of the contraction she was having. "When y'all getting married anyway?" She questioned.

"Actually, our ceremony is next month, October 10th to be exact. It's gonna be quaint but I'll be sure to give you an invitation." She assured Red. "And thank you." Toni continued.

"Honestly, I couldn't think of anyone else I wanted to be here . . . that could be here anyway." Red had sadness in her voice that was clearly recognized by Toni.

She was aware that Red was referring to Romero and she couldn't help but to feel guilt due to the way her past indiscretions had affected other's lives. As hard as she tried, it was more difficult for her to forgive herself than the forgiveness she received from other people.

Toni bought movies to watch and books to read in an effort to distract Red from her pain. They were watching a Kevin Hart comedy stand up when Red began to have complications.

"Something's not right, Toni." Red said seriously, holding her belly.

"What's wrong?" Toni approached the bed with a look of concern.

"I don't hear the baby's heart monitor and he's not moving." Then as if someone stuck her with a hot poker, Red screamed with excruciating agony.

Toni immediately ran out of the room and grabbed the first person in a uniform she saw.

"Please help me, my friend Red, I mean um, Drea Mason needs a doctor!" Toni told the nurse frantically.

"Okay, calm down ma'am, we're gonna take care of her." Just as the nurse finished her sentence, a crew of doctors and nurses rushed into Red's room.

Everything seemed to move in slow motion and Toni's heart began to pound so loudly she barely heard the announcement over the loud speaker.

"Mason, Labor and Delivery three, Code Blue!"

# "911"

The youth program was a success and even ran over about an hour and a half. Services were coming to a close when Ivey, Brandon, and David all received simultaneous 911 text messages which were followed by a text letting them know that Red was having complications with her labor. *Pray for her*, is how she ended her texts.

As soon as Toni's fiancé, David, or Deacon James as the congregation called him, received her text, he immediately announced to the church that he was sending out a special prayer.

"Father God, please bless and protect our sister Drea and her unborn son. We ask that you place your hands on them and guide the hands of the doctors Lord, in the name of your Son we pray, Amen." David prayed.

"Amen." The congregation said in unison.

David handed the services over to another Deacon to close the

ceremony and the three immediately left the church and headed to the
hospital.

Ivey was ahead of the men as she ran down the corridor to the waiting room. Toni was the first person she saw and immediately rushed to embrace her.

"What happened?" Ivey asked Toni as they sat next to one another. Toni was in tears and partially frantic at the thought that Red or her baby was in danger.

"Initially, Red said she wasn't feeling right, but then she lost consciousness and they haven't told me anything. The nurse said she would give me an update, but it's been over an hour." Toni told them literally shaking.

David approached Toni and sat on the other side of her. He embraced her and kissed her on the temple.

"Baby it's gonna be okay. We prayed for her, now we need to trust God, be strong for her, and let his will be done." David told her sounding wiser than his twenty-five years.

All four of them sat and prayed together for what seemed like an eternity. Finally, the nurse that promised to keep Toni updated, entered the waiting room. Toni stood as the nurse approached them with an expression that frightened her.

"We had to perform an emergency C-section because of the baby's heart rate dropping. So the baby is doing well. But we didn't discover the internal bleeding until after the delivery. They're trying to stabilize her now. I know you were here for the delivery, but do you know how to contact her family or the baby's father? We have to be prepared for the worst." The nurse said solemnly.

"I know how to reach her parents, but not the father." Toni said looking down into her lap.

David rubbed the back of her neck. "We'll contact who we can." He told the nurse instead of Toni.

Ivey called Red's mother, Brenda, to inform her of the situation. The conversation was strange to her. She wasn't sure what Red and her mother's relationship was like, but Brenda hardly sounded like a woman that could be possibly losing a daughter. In fact, she was very detached and nonchalant to the point where Ivey wasn't sure if she even planned to come to the hospital.

She hung up the phone with a look of perplexity on her face then she turned to face her family.

"I don't think anyone is coming y'all." She said getting everyone's
attention.

"Whatchu mean?" Toni asked with bewilderment.

"I mean, I don't think Mrs. Mason cares very much. It looks like we may be all she's got."

"But what about the baby?" Toni was concerned.

They all looked at one another with the deepest sympathy, but Toni felt it was not just her duty to be there for Red no matter what; it was also her calling.

Momma Dearest

(Two weeks ago)

Since Raina and Ryan didn't have friends in Chesterfield, Red made sure to take them to visit their grandparents on the Westside of St. Louis. They lived in a rundown duplex that they actually owned and could have had tenants paying them rent. But they were both so caught up in their own vices; they never found time to get their priorities straight.

Red felt she pretty much raised herself, so she had very little respect for either of them outside of the fact that they gave her life. Brenda had been an alcoholic as long as Red could remember. Red was pretty certain that her mother smoked crack as well, but she couldn't prove it. Her dad Rufus was seventeen years older than Brenda and the biggest pushover Red had ever known.

As a child, Red watched her mother cheat and never get caught. She was sure that Rufus was aware of Brenda's whoredom, but just didn't care. Or maybe they had arrangement, but to her, either way it was absolutely dysfunctional.

That dysfunction is what caused her to lash out as a teen and spend a majority of her young life in children's homes. But her strength allowed her to overcome all odds and she managed to go to college and get a degree. If it were not for the tragedy that happened last year, Red was certain that she would still be in New York.

Out of respect, Red would always go inside to say hello to her parents, but she wouldn't stay long. The house was filthy, and it smelled atrocious.

She couldn't stand it under normal circumstances, so her pregnancy made it almost impossible to breath.

When she entered the house she instinctively stopped breathing from her nose. It was her natural reaction when she knew something smelled bad. She walked into the living room to see Rufus doing what he always did, watching TV. She was sure she had seen him in those same clothes for about a week, at least.

"Hi Daddy." Red said as she kept walking and headed to the kitchen.

Rufus didn't even speak; he just waved his hand as she passed. As she entered the kitchen, she wasn't surprised to see Brenda finishing off a bottle of Wild Turkey. Her hair was all over her head and she looked like she was desperate for a bath.

"Hey Momma." Red said dryly.

Brenda turned toward her as she swallowed the last of what was left in the bottle.

"Fuck you want?" Brenda asked rolling her eyes.

"I don't WANT anything." Red rolled her eyes back. "I'll be outside watching the kids." She decided she didn't want to deal with Brenda's bitterness.

Their relationship had always been strained, but after Peaches left all her finances in Red's hands, which totaled over two million dollars in cash and almost a million dollars in property, Brenda had been treating her like a true step-child. Plus, she knew her mother wasn't fit to raise a dog. Red never left Ryan and Raina alone with her and she couldn't understand how Peaches did for so long, let alone a large sum of money.

Red could remember a day when her mother was beautiful. She was light skinned and built like a coke bottle. Peaches got her looks directly from Brenda, body and all. They both had beautiful long hair with natural blonde streaks and light brown eyes. But Brenda let herself go a long time ago. Red was light skinned as well, but she possessed different attributes.

The only weight she gained during her pregnancy was all in her stomach. Otherwise, she was still slim with double D implants. And unlike her sister, Red kept a sew in that hung to the middle of her back. She tried to keep a hair style that would complement her dark cat shaped eyes.

Red sat in her Lexus and watched as Raina and Ryan played with their friends. It brought back memories of when her and Peaches use to play on the same street with Ivey and Toni. She felt a sense of nostalgia at the sight of the old Danes residents down the street. She smiled at the thought.

"I need some money!" The sound of Brenda's voice jolted Red from pleasant childhood memories.

"Momma, I just sent you and Daddy some money. You spent five thousand dollars in less than two weeks? I hope you at least paid y'all's bills." Red said with disgust in her voice and on her face.

Brenda walked off the porch and up to Red's car. Red was embarrassed for her as she walked down the steps barefoot in a dingy tattered moo moo dress. Red couldn't tell if it was supposed to be gray, white, or yellow.

"Who the fuck you talkin' to? I'm still yo momma lil' girl!" Brenda yelled trying to intimidate Red.

"Momma I'm grown and I'm not in your house." Before Red could
finish her thought, Brenda interrupted her.

"You think you better than me? You ain't shit. Yo money, yo car, that house, yo degree, that don't make you nobody. Knowing where you come from makes you somebody and apparently you don't or else you wouldn't treat me like you do." Brenda was in full-fledged guilt trip mode.

But Red didn't care; she started the engine and proceeded to pull
away.

"That's why I should've aborted yo ass!" Brenda yelled in a last
attempt to get Red's attention.

That day, Red decided she would not be going back. She refused to be stressed during her pregnancy and she was not subjecting any of the children to her mother's emotional and psychological abuse. She picked up Raina and Ryan from a few doors down and made plans to enroll the children in a play group in the area where she lived.

"Farewell momma dearest."

Déjà vu


It had been a little over a month since Toni received the peculiar text message from an unrecognized number. But, she was still disturbed none the less.

"BECAUSE OF U, MY LIFE WILL NEVER BE WHAT IT WAS. ENJOY WHAT U HAVE NOW ...I'LL BE BACK!"

Toni had the message still saved in her iPhone. She couldn't imagine
who would still be around to make threats. Peaches was physically unable to send her the message and as far as she knew, everyone else involved in her rape and attempted murder were dead.

She was headed to St. John's Mercy to check on Red and the baby. They finally left the hospital after the doctors were able to stabilize Red. The problem was, Red had lost an enormous amount of blood and was in desperate need of a blood transfusion. Red's blood type was O negative and in short supply.

The only way to be sure she received what she needed, Red would need a member of her family to be a donor. And after Ivey told her about the conversation she had with Brenda, it seemed that it may be almost impossible.

As Toni drove south down Kingshighway headed to highway 40, she noticed a blue Mercedes truck in her rearview mirror. Her heart began to pound, and her hands grew shaky and sweaty. The truck was identical to the truck that had followed her and that she was eventually kidnapped in a year ago. The only time she had been this nervous and afraid was on that gruesome day. She pressed the accelerator in an effort to ditch the truck, but she was unsuccessful.

Toni didn't care if she drew the attention of the police, she actually prayed for it. She whipped in and out of traffic trying to get away. Confusion swept over her.

"I need to see the plates!" She said as she swerved through traffic.

But the front plate was missing and the windows were tinted so dark she couldn't see who was inside.

Finally, she stopped abruptly at a stop sign on Oakland. She felt the truck hit the back of her Camaro. Toni's head hit the steering wheel from the force of her slamming on her brakes. When she got her bearings, and looked in the rearview mirror, the truck wasn't there.

She jumped out of the car and walked to the back of the vehicle; no damage. Then she rubbed her forehead and felt a small knot starting to form. Now she was more confused than before. Was this all just a hallucination? Was she suffering from some form of delayed Post Traumatic Stress Disorder? These questions all floated through her mind before she got back in her car to leave.

"I'm not crazy." Toni said to herself as she got behind the wheel.

She looked in the mirror and the knot was now a full-fledged hickey. "How am I gonna explain this to David?"

David had become especially protective when it came to Toni since her assault, so the last thing she needed was for him to have to worry like she knew he would. Nor did she want him to think she was absolutely insane.

"I'll figure something out." Toni said still talking to herself.

Doing a quick check in her glove box to make sure she had the gun Romero gave her waiting and ready, she prepared to continue her journey to see Red in the hospital. Toni wasn't sure if this was a hallucination or not, but either way she would be prepared.

Something about the incident momentarily triggered 'old' Toni. All she could think was how this time she would be ready if someone came for her. Not once did she stop to pray or ask God for guidance like she had done for the past year. Having David's support usually helped her to stay focused, but today not only was she planning to leave David out of the loop, she planned to protect herself by any means necessary.

Deception 101


Monday mornings were always the hardest for Quitta. Between her and her mother's weekend exploits, neither of them were a pleasure to deal with. They were both usually cranky and hung over, among other things. But this morning, Quitta was especially vibrant.

All she could think about over the weekend was Brandon. She imagined them together and spending time as a couple. As much as she loved Ivey, it didn't stop her fantasies. As a matter of fact, in her young mind, she didn't even connect them to one another until she needed a way to get closer to Brandon.

When she arrived at school, she immediately made her way to Ivey's
office.

"Hi Ivey, um I mean, Mrs. Cameron!" Quitta said all bubbly and excited.

"Hello LaQuitta." Ivey was not receptive to Quitta's energy.

"I just wanted to show you something." Quitta said as she laid a manila folder on Ivey's desk.

"What's this?" Ivey asked as she picked up the folder and thumbed
through its contents.

"It's some artwork. I like to draw, and I remember you mentioning that you and your husband handled the arts and crafts program at the church, and I was kinda interested." Quitta tried to appear as innocent and non-conniving as possible.

"These are really good LaQuitta. You should put a portfolio together. My husband is actually very good at that." Ivey said as she offered Brandon's assistance.

Quitta's heart almost jumped out of her chest when she heard his name, but she had to contain her excitement. She smiled at the thought of her plan coming together.

"No Mrs. Cameron, I don't wanna be a burden to anyone, I'm just interested in the arts and crafts program." Quitta used the best reverse psychology she could muster.

"Nonsense, he would be happy to help you with anything that might
help to better your future." Ivey insisted.

"Are you okay Mrs. Cameron? You don't seem like your normal self." Quitta was fishing.

"Yes, I'm fine, just had a long weekend. Thanks for asking. We have our arts class on Wednesday nights at seven o'clock at the church. You're more than welcomed. Do you mind if I keep this? I can have him start on your portfolio, he'll be really impressed." She said still looking at Quitta's artwork.

"Of course, see you Wednesday." Quitta smiled as she bounced out of the office.

As soon as she hit the hallway she ran into Rocky. "Hey bitch." Rocky gave her the usual greeting.

"What's up, lil' dude." Quitta said trying to be funny as she took notice of Rocky's usual thug fashion.

"Shut up hoe! Whatchu doin' comin' outta there, you in trouble or something?" Rocky asked.

"Nope, I just signed up with Mrs. Cameron and *my man* to do that arts shit they run at the church." Quitta told her.

"Man, what the fuck you up to? You playin' a real dangerous game." Rocky tried to school her.

"I know what I'm doing, don't worry about me!" Quitta began to get irritated by Rocky's judgment.

"I'm just sayin', I know how you get down. And we ain't talkin' about some random mufucka, this is Mrs. Cameron! You need to think about whatchu doin'." Rocky told her right before she entered her homeroom class, leaving Quitta to ponder her deception alone.

"Whatever." Quitta said under her breath.

As right as she knew Rocky was, she didn't care. Her behavior was beyond destructive at this point. It didn't seem to matter who it was, once she set her sights on someone or something, another side of her took over. It was almost like she had to prove to herself that she could have what she wanted, or make whomever she wanted to want her.

To Ivey, Quitta's actions were completely innocent. But the motives behind those actions were less than to be desired.

## Comforter

After the weekend, Ivey had a lot on her mind. Red and the baby were at the top of the list. She was trying to think of a way to approach the Masons about donating blood. When she talked to Red's mother, she couldn't understand the detachment and how a mother could be so evasive about her own child's well-being. However, her focus was on trying to get someone related to Red to come in and donate blood.

While pondering over anything in her power to help Red, Brandon entered their new home with two dozen roses.

"Hey baby, roses for my Ivey." Brandon handed her the flowers as he kissed her on the lips.

I know you've had a rough few days, so I wanted to lift your spirits. I'm not use to you being in a bad mood." Brandon recognized a difference in Ivey ever since they visited Red in the hospital.

Brandon was aware that Ivey was extremely sensitive to other people's situations. That's one of the things he loved about her.

"Thank you, babe. I needed these." She said referring to the roses.

She took a lengthy inhale of the pink roses tipped with red.

"These are beautiful." Ivey felt he needed more than a thank you as appreciation.

She kissed him passionately and began to undress. Ivey had been a virgin until she married Brandon a little over a month ago. But at twenty-two, her sex drive was catching up with her age, and Brandon had no issues with that.

"Can I thank you with this?" Ivey, by this point was butt naked and ready for her husband.

Wearing just a robe gave her easy access to nudity. She pointed to her perfectly shaven vagina. Brandon admired her from head to toe. Her long honey blonde locks hung down her shoulders and to the middle of her back. Her breasts were large and supple, but sat up like she wore and A cup.

Ivey's body was perfect in Brandon's eyes. She had small hips, large breast, a small stomach, and honey brown skin that only made him want a taste of honey. But besides her body, he loved her eyes and dimples. She had slanted honey brown eyes that always mesmerized him.

"Please do." He begged with lust in his eyes as she walked in his direction.

Having no children made it easy for Brandon and Ivey to show their sexual affection whenever, wherever, and however they pleased. Brandon strategically placed the dining room chair before sitting as if he was preparing for a show. Ivey approached him and straddled his lap. As she sat, Brandon caressed every curve of her body.

"Make love to me." She whispered in his ear.

Her body yearned for him. She began to grind on his lap causing his nature to rise. Brandon stood, cupped her cheeks and carried her into the kitchen, then sat her on the marble counter top. She was barely able to control herself. Ivey pulled his shirt over his head between their kisses and caresses.

Brandon had waited over two years to lay with Ivey and it was worth every second. Now, just the anticipation of being with her made him want to burst. He loved her so much, at times he wished he could crawl into her skin, so they would be one.

"I want to taste you." Brandon whispered into her mouth.

Ivey happily obliged him as she lay back on the counter and opened her legs. He buried his face between her thighs and teased her clit with his tongue. Her body reacted as if a jolt of electricity had been sent through it. Moans of ecstasy caused his nature to harden to its peak. He teased her nipples as he sucked her clit and her body shook as he brought her to a climax.

Brandon then released his massive hard on from his jeans and kicked the jeans across the kitchen floor. He wanted to feel Ivey's wetness pulsating from her orgasm. He entered her slowly as her walls tightened around his penis with the rhythm of a heartbeat.

Giving her long slow strokes at first, he watched as her body moved to his rhythm. Then, as if he hit a switch, Ivey's pace started to quicken. She had zoned out into another level of ecstasy. Her body tingled. Sex with Brandon was always beautiful, but this time something was different. Ivey didn't recognize the feeling in her loins. Their strokes got faster and harder.

"Brandon, wait!" Ivey cried.

But he heard nothing but moans of pleasure.

"Oh my God, what's happening?" Ivey wasn't sure how to react to what she felt. "I think I'm cuming!"

"Me too, aaaaauuuggh!" Brandon screamed.

Suddenly a flood of juices gushed from between her thighs.

"What is that? I'm so sorry." She was embarrassed and almost in tears.

Brandon put his arms around her and smiled to himself. He knew she
had nothing to be embarrassed about. Their sex life had just moved up a notch. He felt a sense of pride on the inside. "She's all mine."

Rocky's Road


Her last class was coming to an end and Rocky had already decided that she was not in the mood for Quitta. She felt Quitta's constant antics to get the attention of the opposite sex was a cry for help in the wrong direction. Rocky was only sixteen, but her insight on life was very different than other girls her age.

Quitta, actually reminded her of her own mother Gabriella. She watched her mother jump from man to man, and they usually overlapped one another. Not to mention, none of them were ever considerable as a father figure. So Rocky never trusted them, especially around her little sisters Laniah and Mariah.

Gabriella was originally from Puerto Rico and moved to the U.S. as a child with her mother when she ran away from Gabriella's abusive father. She always rebelled, and her behavior was usually frowned upon by her devout Catholic mother, Isabelle

Santiago or Mama Isa, as Rocky and her sisters called their grandmother.

Mama Isa was more of a mother than a grandmother considering Gabriella was absent most of the time. They usually saw her on the weekends between her barrage of dates, or in the mornings on the way to school, if she happened to fall asleep on the couch because she was too intoxicated to make it to her bedroom.

When the bell rang Rocky didn't hesitate, she immediately made a beeline for the east exit to the school. She walked directly to Northview Elementary to pick up her twin siblings like she did every day. They actually depended on Rocky more than anyone outside of Mama Isa. She stood in front of the school until she saw the seven-year-old versions of herself appear in the doorway.

"Kelly!" Mariah screamed when she saw her big sister.

She started running and Laniah followed suit. They both hugged her waist on opposite sides of her body.

"How was school?" Rocky asked them when they let her go.

"It was okay." Laniah said. "Good." Mariah followed up.

They were identical twins and only Rocky could tell them apart; they even fooled Mama Isa from time to time. The girls were as close as sisters could be. They even created their own language so no one, not even Rocky, could understand them.

"What y'all want to eat?" Rocky asked them, pulling a wad of money from her pocket.

"McDonalds!" They sang.

Rocky would do whatever it took to take care of her sisters; hustle, steal, and even kill if she had to.

"Okay, let's go." They walked to McDonalds about ten minutes away.

After the girls ate their meals, Rocky bought them shakes and took them to the playground; that was their routine. Laniah and Mariah were her first priority, and making sure she had money to take care of them was her second.

"Can we see Mama today?" Laniah asked Rocky looking up at her with sad almond eyes.

"I don't know Niah, I hope so. I'm sure she misses us too. She just gets busy sometimes." Rocky lied.

She looked down at them both and couldn't understand how her mother could neglect them. They were beautiful little girls with angelic hearts. They both wore one long ponytail that hung down their backs. All three girls were bi-racial, Puerto Rican because of Gabriella and Black because of whoever they're fathers were. But neither of the girls knew their fathers and Rocky never trusted men because of the role models her mother put before them.

The three sisters walked home and talked about their day. This was always the highlight of Rocky's day. She couldn't believe how fast her little sisters had grown up and how intelligent they were. Despite the fact that Gabriella was almost non-existent, both girls maintained straight As and Bs, and were always on the honor roll. Rocky kept her grade point average above a 3.0 and had aspirations of becoming a restaurant owner.

The girls approached the two-family flat that they shared with Mama Isa. But today something was different. Rocky heard yelling from the downstairs unit where she and her sisters lived, so she took them to the upstairs unit with their grandmother until she knew things were safe. Then, she came back downstairs to find out what was going on.

She saw an old school Cadillac Seville in front of the house, but she didn't recognize it and there were still loud voices coming from downstairs. Rocky quietly entered the living room and saw a large dark-skinned man, about six-foot three or so, towered over her petite Puerto Rican princess of a mother. Gabriella looked like a mouse in the corner as he roared like a lion, and she was afraid to move.

"What the fuck you think you doin' bitch? I got a business to run and
you can't be runnin' off and shit!" His voice was deep and seemed to make the room vibrate.

"I'm sorry, but I needed to come check on my kids." Gabriella said with a slight Spanish accent.

"Didn't I tell you if you crossed me I would fuck you up? You think this a joke? Did you forget who I am?" His voice seemed to go up half an octave with every question.

He loomed over her five-foot two-inch frame as she stood pale, shivering, and afraid. Rocky wasn't sure what to do, but she knew she wouldn't allow this to go on much longer.

"No Papi!" She wept.

Gabriella stood in the comer with her hands in front of her face like she anticipated a blow.

"What fuckin' kids anyway? I don't see no damn kids!" He continued with his intimidation while looking around the room.

That was Rocky's cue. She stepped into the living room just as he stopped talking.

"Mama, what's going on, you okay?" Rocky said hoping to interrupt this interrogation.

But before Gabriella could respond, the big black man that looked more like a Sasquatch than a person, wearing an oversized mink in 72° weather, turned to look at Rocky. His nostrils were flaring, and his eyes seemed black.

"Damn baby girl, what do we have here?" He looked her up and down like the pervert she's sure he was.

No matter how many layers of clothing she wore, he could still see the 36-24-40 shape on her five-foot four-inch body.

"Mama are you okay?" Rocky asked again.

"Yes Kelly, I'm okay. Go to Mama Isa's, I'll come get you in a little bit." Gabriella said with pleading green eyes.

By that time, Rocky and the man she only knew as a pervert were staring each other directly in the eyes.

"Naw, she can stay. Come here beautiful; let me talk to you for a minute." The pervert better known as Smiley said to Gabriella and Rocky, but he was walking in Rocky's direction.

"No Smiley!" Gabriella said as she walked up and grabbed his arm, standing up to him for the first time. "That's my baby!"

She barely finished her sentence before Smiley turned with the force of a bulldozer, at least to a woman as small as Gabriella, and slapped her in her slender, petite face with the back of his massive hand. The side of her head hit the comer of the mantle and her body fell to the floor like a ragdoll. Rocky immediately ran to her mother's side and for the first time she realized that her mother actually did love them, regardless to what demons she was battling.

"Tell that bitch to call me when she wake up." Smiley demanded as he hurriedly abandoned the domestic situation.

"Mama wake up! Mama!" Rocky continued to shake her unresponsive mother.

Rocky sat silently and held her mother trying to feel a pulse. After about twenty seconds she screamed again.

"MAMA!!"

But there was no answer from Gabriella's lifeless body.

Father Knows Best


Ivey and Toni sat at the dining room table at Ivey's preparing a proposal for their non-profit organization. They sat and worked silently. Unbeknownst to them, they were actually thinking about the same thing, Red.

It had only been a couple of days, but every time they went to visit, Red was growing weaker. The baby however was doing fine with the exception of not being able to bond with family. Ivey and Toni even considered the possibility of donating themselves until the doctor made them aware that with Red's blood type, finding a donor outside the family would be difficult.

"So, what are we gonna do?" Ivey said breaking the silence.

"I mean, what can we do? Didn't you say Brenda acted like she didn't care?" Toni reminded her.

"Yes, but there's gotta be someone." Ivey sounded defeated.

"I tell you what, I'm gonna call Daddy and see if he can talk some
sense into Rufus." Toni said.

"God luck with that, because good luck won't help you. You know Brenda's had control over that man since we were little. He acts like he's getting beat." Ivey joked seriously.

"I know right?" Toni laughed. "Between Brenda and the way Red use to clown, I'm surprised that poor man is still alive." She finished.

"I think it'll help persuade him if he hears it from a father that went through something similar." Ivey was referring to Toni's bout with death a year ago.

"Me too, but it's a shame they can't just test Peaches. That would
make this a lot easier." Toni said.

"No, it's a shame that her own parents haven't run to the hospital to help their daughter or check on their grandchild!" Ivey was extremely irritated with the whole situation and Red's parents.

"Calm down Chickadee. I'll talk to Daddy and we'll go from there. Okay li' gir'?" Toni knew Ivey hated when she called her that, but she also knew it was only to lift her spirits.

"Whatever heffa." Ivey joked while laughing at her big sister.

Ivey was ecstatic that she finally truly had her sister in her life. They continued with their 50lc3 application for their non-profit organization for youths, while Ivey prayed that Toni's idea to get their father to convince Rufus to donate to Red would work.

Later that day
(Randy & Regina's)

Toni decided to go see her dad about the Red situation. Randy and Toni's relationship had done a complete 180°. Unlike before, Toni visited her father and his wife Regina regularly.

Toni had issues with her dad for years after her mother Lois and his divorce. But her feelings for him deteriorated further after Lois died of Lupus when she was eighteen and Ivey was sixteen and they were sent to live with their maternal grandmother Mee Maw Gloria.

But Toni's near-death encounter made them both realize that life was entirely too short to take the people they loved for granted any longer. And even though Regina could never replace Lois, Toni even nurtured their relationship as well. She realized now that the way she lived before was not life, she only existed. Now she was living a life that consisted of real love and a chance for happiness; although, she had yet to tell anyone about the blue Mercedes truck.

Fall in St. Louis was usually beautiful, but today it was raining cats and dogs. Toni pulled up to her dad's house in West County. Their house was beautiful. If nothing else, Regina had excellent taste. The house resembled a small villa on the outside and the inside was immaculately decorated in a Victorian fashion.

Before becoming an active part of their lives, Toni assumed Regina was a gold digger. But she soon found out that couldn't be further from the truth. Her dad worked for Boeing as long as Toni could remember, but Regina was a nurse anesthetist and was the head nurse in the anesthesiology department at Barnes Jewish Hospital, and she actually made more money than Randy.

Toni was glad she wore a ponytail as she high tailed it through the rain and up to the door. After ringing the doorbell, Regina greeted her with a hug and a towel.

Regina physically, was the exact opposite of Toni's mother, Lois. She was around five-foot two, light skinned, and extremely thin. Toni thought she actually had a nice shape; it was just very petite. Also, she had hazel eyes and sandy brown, shoulder length, naturally curly hair. Toni considered her "cute" at best.

"Hurry in here out of that rain sweetheart." Regina sounded like the whitest white woman with perfect grammar and diction. "Here's a towel, take off those shoes and dry off. You could catch pneumonia in this type of weather." Regina said sounding like a mother.

She never actually had children of her own. But now that Toni had allowed them into her life, although late, she tried to be the best mother figure she could for Toni and Ivey both.

"How are you?" Regina asked.

"I'm doing well, thank you." Toni asked reciprocating the politeness. "Where's daddy?" Toni asked looking for a sign of her father's presence.

"He's in the study, he's expecting you." Regina pointed Toni in the direction of the room her father occupied.

Toni stood in the doorway watching her father. She looked at this slender six-foot three inch physique and tried to think back to a time before his hair and mustache were gray. Even though he was getting older, Toni thought her dad was still a handsome man.

"Hi daddy."

"Hey baby girl!" He said with a raspy tone sounding excited to see her.

"Whatchu doin'?" Toni asked giving him small talk at first.

"Just catching up on some work, but I always got time for you. What's up?" Randy put his work to the side on his desk.

"Well, I told you about what's going on with Red right?" Toni reminded him.

"Right."

"Well, I need you to talk to Rufus about donating blood for her. Brenda acts like she could care less and unfortunately she has him under her thumb. So I figured if you talk to him, he may come to his senses." Toni explained.

"Honey, this is not our business." Randy wanted to stay as far away from the Masons as possible.

"But what about the baby? Is it that easy for you to just dismiss somebody's life? Have you even thought about Ryan and

Raina and who will take care of them?" Toni came with a barrage of questions that triggered old feelings about her father.

Randy leaned back in his office chair and thought very carefully about what to say next. Toni stood with her arms across her chest in protest.

"Exactly how am I supposed to convince someone to care if they
don't? I'm not a magician."

"No daddy, but you are a father." Toni had softened her tone and looked at him intensely.

Randy felt the guilt of his past rushing over him like constant clips of a tragic film.

"Okay baby, I'll talk to him . . . but I can't promise anything. And I'm sorry for being dismissive. Believe me; I do understand how this affects everyone." He extended his arms for a hug.

The last thing he wanted was to return to the relationship as it was before. Toni was still on the defensive, but she reluctantly approached her father for a return hug.

"Thank you daddy." Toni had less than no enthusiasm in her voice.

"Honey, I know more about these people than I care to, and I pretty
much already know the outcome. But for you, I will talk to them both, okay?" Randy assured her. "I love you, I would do anything for you." He followed up.

Her heart was lightened before she responded.

"I love you too Daddy. And really, thank you." She smiled at him. "Keep me posted on the outcome. Remember this is a time sensitive issue, so as soon as possible, okay?" She all but begged.

Randy gave her an assuring smile before turning to go through his roll-a-dex to find the Mason's phone number.

Toni decided to leave the room, so he could have the privacy he needed to have a mono e mono heart to heart with Rufus. The last thing she heard as she exited the room was, "Hello, may I speak with Rufus please?"

## Tomorrow Mourning

It had been a few days and Quitta hadn't seen or heard from Rocky. She even stopped by Ivey's office at school to inquire about her whereabouts. But all she was told is that Rocky would be back next week, so she decided that day she would try to call her to see what's going on.

As soon as she walked in the door from school, she could tell her mother was on a rampage of some sort. "Probably some nigga." Quitta thought. Gwen was already cursing under her breath when Quitta entered the kitchen.

"This is some bullshit." Gwen mumbled with her back to Quitta.

"Hi momma." Quitta said dryly.

Gwen didn't respond and Quitta proceeded to grab a snack and headed to her room. She was actually relieved that Gwen decided to keep her emotions to herself, otherwise she would've taken her issues out on Quitta.

When she got to her room, she retrieved her Galaxy Note 2 from her Louis Vuitton backpack. She called Rocky and the phone seemed to ring forever. Just as she was about to hang up, she thought she heard a voice.

"Rocky?" Quitta said making sure she wasn't mistaken.

After a few seconds of silence someone finally spoke.

"Yeah it's me." Rocky sounded like she hadn't used her voice in
months.

It was raspy and it cracked. She was breathy and Quitta could barely hear her. To Quitta, she didn't sound like herself.

"Where you been; I been lookin' for yo ass in the daytime with a flashlight?" Quitta asked jokingly.

"I don't really wanna talk now Quitta." This time she could hear the
pain in Rocky's voice.

"What's wrong Rock?" Quitta was insistent on finding out what was
going on.

The phone line went silent again. She decided to give Rocky a chance to answer before she got impatient. She heard a sigh, and then what she thought was a slight whimper.

"Rocky, talk to me! What's going on friend?" Quitta begged for an
answer.

"My Mama is dead." Rocky almost whispered.

Quitta barely heard her, but she understood what she said and refused to make her repeat it. She wanted to know what happened, but she was afraid to ask about that too.

Rocky cleared her throat. "The funeral is tomorrow. Do you think your mom will let you go with me?" Rocky needed Quitta's friendship and was glad she reached out to her.

"I'll be there. What time do we leave?" Quitta was going to be there for her friend no matter what her mom said.


The next day

Rocky told Quitta that the limo left at ten in the morning, so she arrived at nine thirty just in case Rocky needed help with the girls. She knocked on the door and Mama Isa answered. She didn't even say hello before immediately dismissing Quitta.

"Raquel is leaving now." Mama Isa said with a heavy Spanish accent.

"Hello Mrs. Santiago, I'm so sorry for your loss. But I'm going to the
funeral with Rocky." Quitta tried to explain.


Just as Rocky walked outside on the porch, Mama Isa gave a grunt of disapproval.

"Como pueda u respeto funeral de su madre que esa forma de vida
aqui?" She spat at Rocky.

"Mama Isa, what lifestyle? Quitta is my friend and I'm not being disrespectful to Mama!" Rocky was tired, tired of her grandmother's disapproval, and tired of trying to be accepted by someone that should love her unconditionally.

The husky Puerto Rican woman stood with her hands on her hips and a scowl on her face.

"I forbid it!" Mama Isa said before she stomped back into the house.

Rocky felt defeated as she sat on the top step of the porch and rested her face in her hands. Quitta sat next to her grieving friend and tried to console her.

"I hate her." Rocky said through clenched teeth.

"Don't say that, you don't mean it." Quitta told her.

"She hates me. Well she acts like it anyway. My mama accepted me for who I am. Mama Isa doesn't love you unless you live by her rules, just like she did my mama." Rocky was starting to break down at the thought that she wouldn't have a shoulder to cry on now that Quitta couldn't attend the funeral with her.

Quitta put her arm around Rocky's shoulders and tried to relieve her mourning. She felt bad for her. Even though her relationship with Gwen was as dysfunctional as they came, Quitta couldn't imagine her life without her. Gwen was her mother, good or bad, and although she empathized with Rocky, she did not want to experience that kind of loss. But she would be there for Rocky as much as she could.

"Let me know when it's over, I'll be here when you get back." She assured Rocky. "I love you friend."

Rocky looked up at her long and hard, and she realized Quitta was being genuine. With all she was dealing with, it warmed her heart to know she had a real friend in Quitta.

"Thank you and I love you too."

"WTF"

"I don't know who the fuck you think I am, but I don't chase niggas!" Gwen roared through the phone into Clarence's voicemail before she hung up.

It was the tenth time or so that she had called him after he stood her
up four days ago. They were supposed to meet at their usual spot, but this time he instructed the front desk to give her a key because he would be late. After falling asleep and waking up at six the next morning, Clarence still had not shown up and Gwen was pissed. What was worse is that he hadn't even attempted to contact her.

"Fuck him!" Gwen said while laying her iPhone on the counter in the kitchen.

She was so upset that she didn't even address Quitta when she came in from school the day before. And she still hadn't spoken to her. Gwen was cleaning the kitchen and preparing to cook dinner when Quitta walked in.

"Hi Momma." Quitta attempted for the second day in a row to get a response.

"Hey Quitta." Gwen actually responded, but sounded like she would have rather not.

Quitta went directly to grab some apples for snack so she could retreat to her room to absorb all that Rocky had told her and all that transpired after the funeral. Quitta was still in disbelief that Gabriella's murderer and pimp had the audacity to ride past Rocky's home. She would never forget his face or Rocky's emotional reaction to him.

Plus, the last thing she needed or wanted was a confrontation with her mother. Their disagreements were usually a deflection from something else and non-related to Quitta. Gwen just used whatever her real issue was as a catalyst to take her disappointments out on Quitta.

"Where you been?" Quitta was in a mild state of shock at the thought that Gwen might have actually cared.

"I was at Rocky's." Quitta answered still cutting up apples to dip into her bowl of crunchy peanut butter.

"You mean that gay girl?" Gwen's voice was full of accusation.

"Momma, I don't know or care who that girl is sleeping with, she's just my friend. All that other stuff ain't my business. Besides, her mother was murdered in front of her almost a week ago, so I hardly think that her sexual preference is relevant now!" Quitta was highly upset and emotional, but tried to control the volume in her voice.

Gwen was in shock at the news, but she also found herself feeling sorry for Quitta and her friend.

"I'm sorry to hear that. We will have to send flowers and a card of condolences." Gwen was always absolutely appropriate in every situation, with the exception of Quitta. "Are you okay?" Gwen asked her sounding like a real mother.

"Yeah, I'm alright, thanks for asking." Quitta was used to her mother's random acts of kindness, so she didn't feel special today.

Quitta headed to her room as planned and left Gwen alone with her
thoughts. Gwen thought about Rocky's mother and tried to remember what Gabriella looked like although she had only seen her a few times. But she was suddenly jarred from her attempt at recollection by the sound of her phone ringing.

*Let's Get it On* by Marvin Gaye played as she looked down at the phone trying to decide if she wanted to answer.

"Hello." She said making her decision.

"Hey baby." Clarence said in a smooth, low voice.

"Don't baby me negro!" Gwen's tone was not so smooth and low. "Did you just realize you stood me up, or do you feel so entitled that you can do whatever you want?" Gwen barked.

The line was quiet momentarily.

"You finished? I want you to be able to vent, you have every right to be upset." Clarence told her with compassion.

"Is that supposed to be an apology?" Gwen's voice was loaded with attitude.

"No, the apology comes with dinner." His voice seemed to melt through the phone lines and caress her eardrum as she tried to remain upset.

"Dinner, you mean room service?" She said sarcastically.

"I'm taking you out to dinner. That is if you'll accept my invitation?" As Clarence spoke, she almost forgot the night she spent alone and the last few days she called him non-stop with no response, but she didn't.

"Why did you stand me up, and where have you been? I'm supposed to be 'yours' right? I don't take very kindly to being ignored." Gwen tried to stand her ground, no matter how weak she felt on the inside.

"Some important business came up and I couldn't be distracted. I have to be discrete with company information, so I can't disclose too much. Just trust me when I say, I would have rather been with you." Clarence remained vague but tried to sound sincere. "Can I take you to dinner please?" He tried again to convince her.

Gwen sighed long and hard.

"You won't get a third time to piss me off, so you better make it count." She decided that whatever it was he was doing, he would have to respect her.

She felt something; more than she wanted to. But one thing was for sure, she refused to show any emotional weakness; at least not yet anyway.

Organized Chaos


While the arts and crafts program died down at God's Kingdom Church, Quitta sulked in the auditorium thinking about Rocky.

"We missed you in class." Quitta heard the baritone voice of Brandon approaching.

"I'm sorry; I've got some things on my mind. I'm glad you missed me though." She was feeling down about Rocky, but she couldn't help but take advantage of an opportunity to flirt with Brandon. "How's the portfolio coming along?" Quitta inquired.

"Oh, I'm glad you asked." Brandon unzipped his leather briefcase to retrieve the most professional portfolio she'd ever seen.

"Thank you so much! I can't believe this is my stuff!" She couldn't be more excited if she tried.

She jumped up from the bench and hugged Brandon. At first, the hug
was innocent and elementary. Then subtly, Quitta began to sensually caress him. Brandon quickly discontinued her embrace and slightly pushed her away as he removed himself from her reach.

"What are you doing LaQuitta?" He was concerned and confused at the same time.

"I just wanted to pay you for all of your help?" She said like she
couldn't understand his objection. "I've seen how you look at me Brandon,
I know you want me." She began to invade his personal space again.

Brandon grabbed both her shoulders as if to shake some sense into her.

"Listen!" His initial tone startled her, and he noticed, so Brandon
softened his voice as he continued. "Even if you weren't a minor and too young for me to even consider a relationship with, I am very happily married. So, as the adult in this situation, I have to tell you this is absolutely inappropriate." He said with a stern voice.

Quitta stood like a deer caught in headlights. She backed away from Brandon as if she had suddenly come to her senses. And with one deep breath, she broke down into tears.

"I'm sorry, please don't tell Mrs. Cameron. I don't know what I was thinking!" She sat down on the bench and hid her face in her hands out of shame. "I was just so happy about my pictures." Her comment was muffled, but he understood.

He had been dealing with troubled teens for the past few years and could recognize when they were starved for attention. Suddenly, he began to feel sorry for her. Brandon stood beside her and touched her shoulder.

"This is just between me and you. But you have to promise never to do that again." He told her with a hint of reprimand in his voice.

"I promise."

"I'm ready when you are." The sound of Ivey's voice echoed from a few rows away.

Both Quitta and Brandon were startled momentarily. Quitta jumped from her seat like it was on fire.

"Oh, hi Mrs. Cam . . . Ivey." Quitta said nervously, but recovered to her normal self in record time to Brandon's surprise.

"Hello LaQuitta, how are you?" Ivey asked her.

"I'm doing alright, I guess."

"What about Rocky, is she still coming back to school next week?" As Ivey and Quitta conversed, Brandon was amazed at how Quitta managed to pretend like she hadn't done anything.

She acted as if the last five minutes had not taken place. Brandon felt she deserved an Oscar for her performance.

"I'll be in the car babe." Brandon interrupted.

He couldn't take another second, he just let them continue their exchange and he went to his Impala. He was in awe of Quitta's sudden change of emotion. He felt it was a potentially dangerous situation and had to decide if Ivey needed to know what happened just yet. One thing was for sure, he could see through Quitta like saran wrap, and she could not be trusted.

## Questionable

Clarence made good on his apology dinner and Gwen was feeling slightly renewed in her faith in him. He made sure to have gifts and money to appease her pride as well as her greed. However, she was still questionable about his life outside of the time he spent with her.

Gwen had tried to overcome her reputation of being naive since she was young. Her parents were over forty when she was born, and she lived a sheltered existence in Des Moines, Iowa as a preacher's kid. Then she moved to Missouri to attend Southeast Missouri State. Moving to St. Louis exposed her to a faster pace of life and men like Clarence. So, she tried to stay on her toes.

After the apology dinner, they started to actually make public appearances. But they were both still very discrete about where they lived. Gwen knew her reason, but she couldn't understand Clarence's need for secrecy. She even paid close attention to his ring finger and phone interactions. So far so good; there was no tan line or private phone calls up until this point.

Gwen didn't trust people because they always seemed to disappoint her; her ex-husband Franklin, a number of her exes, and even Quitta. So needless to say, she kept her guard on ten. But Clarence was slowly breaking down that guard.

Tonight, he planned a dinner at Chase Park Plaza, where he had also reserved a suite for the night. Gwen wore her sexiest black dress and four-inch pumps. She wanted to look good enough to eat, literally.

They met at the bar inside the hotel. When she approached, Gwen was impressed by what she saw. Clarence wore a navy three-piece suit and silk tie. He looked like a GQ model with smooth dark skin and groomed to perfection.

She walked up behind him. "You're the finest man in here tonight." She said catching him off guard.

"Well you my dear, look good enough to eat." He said returning the compliment.

Gwen smiled when she got her desired reaction. They had a few drinks at the bar and enjoyed each other's company. Clarence was all gentlemen. He pulled out her chair, held her hand when they walked, and she was sure if needed, he would have laid his jacket over a puddle. He was proving to be everything she wanted in a man.

They sat across the dinner table from one another, silent for a moment.

"So, what am I missing?" Gwen broke the silence.

"What do you mean?" Clarence asked.

"I mean, you seem too good to be true. With the exception of me not knowing where you live of course." She said.

"Well, I told you, I'm very careful when it comes to inviting anyone to my home. I've had some bad experiences. And I don't know where you live either little lady, so how should I feel about that?" Clarence reminded her.

"I have a daughter and I told you, I don't introduce her to every man I
meet." This time Gwen was doing the reminding.

"I completely understand that, which is why I haven't pushed the issue." He told her with a tone that said she should do the same.

"You're right, and neither will I." She smiled and decided to change the subject.

They talked about everything from politics to religion, and Gwen was impressed that he could actually keep up. She was so used to dealing with men that had so little of what she was looking for in a man that she was beginning to settle. But not anymore, she thought as she admired Clarence and his intellect.

"What's up King?" A tall, well dressed, light skinned man said as he approached the table.

"Hey JB, what's goin' on man? Long time no see." Clarence seemed
surprised and excited.

"Yeah you know they had me down for a while, and these bitches ain't doin' they job? JB said looking around the restaurant.

"JB." Clarence cut him off. "This is my lady Gwen. Gwen this is an old friend of mine, JB." He introduced them.

Gwen was disgusted by his use of the word bitch, but she extended her hand anyway.

"Nice to meet you." Gwen said dryly.

"Hey, how you doin'?" JB said seeming uninterested while leaving her hand in the air.

"So, is it true?" JB asked Clarence.

The look Clarence gave him could've been read a few ways in Gwen's mind. He was either very confused, or he was giving him a sign to shut the hell up. His next move would tell her exactly what he meant.

"Baby, can you excuse me for a minute." Clarence pulled JB to the side without waiting for Gwen's response.

She watched as their interactions and body language quickly changed from friendly to argumentative. Gwen strained her ears to try and get some idea of what was going on. Then Clarence abruptly ended the conversation and walked back to the table.

"Nigga, I was tryna make sure yo stable gone be taken care of, fuck you!" JB said making a small scene as he exited the five-star restaurant.

"What was that all about?" Gwen asked Clarence as he returned to his seat.
"Nothing, don't worry about that baby." He said.

"So, am I supposed to just ignore everything?" Gwen didn't feel comfortable anymore.

Clarence was extremely agitated, and it was visible. And along with his mood, his demeanor had changed as well.

"Didn't I say don't worry about that or are you hard of hearing or something?" He snapped at her.

Gwen sat her glass on the table and leaned back in her seat. She saw something in his eyes she had never seen before. Silent at first, she watched his expression soften before she spoke.

"I'm leaving." She told him as she stood up and grabbed her clutch.

"Wait a minute, I'm sorry!" He tried to stop her but it was too late.

Gwen walked out to valet and gave a young white man in a red vest her ticket and a tip. As she waited, she pondered over the last few minutes and how it all changed so quickly. Also, this was the second time he momentarily stepped out of character and it bothered her.

"You leavin' so soon? What happened, King didn't live up to your
expectations?"

Gwen turned to see JB standing outside smoking a cigarette.

"You need to choose me, I run a better stable anyway."

Gwen was grateful that the valet pulled up when he did. JB made her uncomfortable, plus she didn't know what he was talking about. To her, this entire evening had been strange. And just when she thought it couldn't get any stranger, she got a text message from Clarence as she got in her car.

**Clarence:** I TOLD YOU, YOU BELONG TO ME NOW. SO THE CAT AND MOUSE GAMES ARE OVER!!! THERE IS NOWHERE YOU CAN GO THAT I WON'T FIND YOU, EVEN HOME!!

Gwen wasn't afraid, but she had never dealt with anything quite like this before. She realized now that whoever Clarence King was, she didn't know him at all. But her advantage in this situation was, is that he didn't know her either.

Trust Issues

When David and Toni entered Red's hospital room, they were not only surprised to see the baby, but Red seemed to be doing a thousand percent better. Toni gave a sigh of relief when she saw that Red was no longer pale, weak, and exhausted. She was even breast feeding.

"Oh wow, you look great mommy. I guess my dad came through?" Toni said as she greeted Red with the motion of a hug, so she wouldn't crush the baby.

Toni had actually gone to the nursery on several occasions to see the baby, but she hadn't noticed until today how much he resembled Romero. He had the same deep-set eyes, chiseled nose, and thick lips. It appeared the only thing he got from Red was her color.

"To be honest Toni, I haven't seen either of my parents. So, I'm not sure where the blood came from. They just told me that someone with my blood type donated, and that's all I know." Red was baffled but grateful to whomever it was.

She could actually feel the life slipping from her before the transfusion. And being too tired to nurse or hold her baby made her depressed, on top of everything else.

"Well, I'm happy to see you back in the land of the living, you had my baby ready to steal you parent's blood in their sleep." David joked, and they all laughed.

"I appreciate this woman. No one could have ever told me that we would be here, but I'm glad we are." Red said sincerely giving Toni an endearing look.

"Girl stop being all mushy and let me hold that baby!"

As she drove home, Toni felt that God had answered her prayers. She was feeling joyful on the inside and David could tell that her mood was different than when they came.

"I told you all you have to do is trust him, right?" David said, referring to God as if he could read her mind.

"I know baby, and I'm really working on my faith. I'm just glad I have you to keep me grounded." She smiled.

"And I'm happy to be here, but Toni you must develop a faithful relationship with God. You have to trust him even when he's not moving as fast as you want him to. And remember, the stronger your faith, the more Satan tries to destroy it." He told her, almost preaching.

They were riding through Forest Park and almost to Toni's loft when her phone vibrated indicating a text message.

"I SEE YOU BITCH!"

She looked at David, then back at her phone. She wanted to be sure this wasn't a hallucination. Just as she thought, the text message was as real as she was.

"What's the matter?" David questioned, noticing how uncomfortable
she had suddenly become.

"Um." She said nervously. "I haven't been completely honest with you David." Toni admitted. "I've been getting strange text messages for a little over a month; threatening messages." She explained.

"Why haven't you told me?" He was concerned about her ability to
be so secretive for so long.

"I don't know. I guess I was afraid you wouldn't want the drama in your life." Toni tried to make her reasoning make sense to even her.

"I want you in my life, and I'll deal with whatever I have to, to make that happen. Don't you trust me by now?" David burned a whole in the side of her face with his stare.

"Yes, but."

"But nothing. We're a few weeks from being husband and wife, but you still treat me like an outsider." He was beginning to get upset.

Before Toni was able to say another word, she noticed the blue Mercedes truck in her rearview mirror.

"Baby, I think we're being followed. Don't tum around." Toni told
him.

"But who would be following you?" David was confused.

"Honestly, I don't know, but this is the second time I've seen this
truck behind me." Toni said not mentioning the small fender bender.

"Maybe it's a coincidence."

"Or, maybe it's the same truck that pulled up to my loft the day I was kidnapped." She said defensively. "But how?" Now she was confused.

They hadn't noticed that during their chat, the truck had pulled right
behind them. Just as Toni looked in the mirror again, BAM! The truck rear ended the small Camaro causing Toni to lose control for a few seconds. The car swerved just a little before Toni hit the gas to get away from the maniac behind the wheel.

POW!

The sound of a gunshot rang into the air. Toni's heart was beating so hard and fast, she thought she would go into cardiac arrest.

POW!

This time Toni's back window shattered. She finally made it to a
main street when the shooting stopped, and the truck disappeared. With glass everywhere, Toni quickly pulled over.

"Are you okay?" She asked David through heavy breathing. She looked over to see David unconscious and bleeding.

"DAVID NOOO!!!!"

## Return to Sender

After being rejected by Brandon, Quitta's agenda had changed. She wasn't used to rejection on any level and was furious that she couldn't have at least some of what she wanted. She had actually seduced several men in her short life. The offer of oral pleasure would usually get any man's attention. And with the exception of a few pedophiles, including Gwen's ex, no one could tell how old she actually was.

She arrived at school early and went directly to Ivey's office. "Good morning Mrs. Cameron, I just wanted to return this." Quitta handed Ivey the portfolio Brandon put together.

"I don't understand, this belongs to you?" Ivey had question in her voice.

"I just feel like I owe something for this. Something this professional can't be free." Quitta's humility touched Ivey's heart.

"Your work deserves professionalism." Ivey assured her.

"Well I hope Mr. Cameron feels the same way." Quitta's display of concern bothered Ivey.

"What do you mean?" Ivey asked.

"Nothing." Quitta said quickly as if she were hiding something.
Ivey couldn't understand Quitta's sudden mood change, so she just chalked it up to teenage hormones.

"Well if you have anything you want to discuss, I'm here, okay?" Ivey assured her.

"Okay." Quitta responded looking toward the floor.

"Is there something wrong LaQuitta?" Ivey was very concerned by her actions.

She didn't respond.

"LaQuitta?" Ivey pushed for a response.

When Quitta lifted her eyes from the floor, they were full of tears. "Oh my goodness, LaQuitta what's wrong?" Ivey's level of concern went from zero to ten.

"I'm sorry Mrs. Cameron, I didn't mean for any of this to happen." Quitta covered her face with her hands in shame.

Ivey walked over to her and walked her to the chair in front of Ivey's
desk.

"Calm down honey. Take a deep breath and tell me what's wrong."

84

Ivey walked around her desk and sat across from Quitta, giving her undivided attention.

She was concerned about her sudden outburst of emotion. Quitta
continued to sob into her hands, and then she began to speak.

"I told him no. I mean I tried to anyway. But he just kept grabbing me and telling me that it's the least I can do, and stuff like that. I was afraid, so I pretended to like his touches, so I could get away. Then he started to kiss me and holding me real tight, and he wouldn't let go!" Quitta began to become frantic like she was living the story as she told it. "So, I kicked him then he got mad and grabbed my shoulders. I was just happy you walked in when you did." She added.

"Glad I walked in, what do you mean?" Ivey questioned her.

Quitta collected herself and stood up from the chair.

"You know what, I've said too much. I shoulda just kept this to myself, I don't want any trouble." Quitta said wiping her tears as she tried to hightail it out of Ivey's office.

"Freeze!" Ivey's tone made Quitta stop in her tracks. "I can't help you if you don't talk to me LaQuitta. Now, who did these things to you?" The room was silent. They looked one another directly in the eyes. Quitta walked back to the chair and sat. She appeared to be in total despair. Finally, Quitta took a long, hard, deep breath before she finally responded. "It was Brandon."

Homeward Bound


Today, Red and Romero Jr., were being released from the hospital. She was excited for several reasons. First of all, she couldn't wait to get back to the comfort of her own home. She felt like she had been hospitalized for months, but it had only been two weeks.

Secondly, she missed Ryan and Raina terribly. She talked to them on the phone almost every day, but she couldn't wait to see their sweet little faces.

Red moved around the room slowly gathering her and the baby's belongings. She smelled all of little RJ's clothing, inhaling his tiny essence. She never felt this way about anyone or anything. Her maternal instinct seemed naturally imbedded, unlike her mother and Peaches. All she wanted to do was love and protect her tiny bundle of joy. He had only been on earth two weeks, and she couldn't imagine her life without him.

"There's your mommy." The nurse baby talked as she wheeled the basinet into the room. "He was getting fussy, I figured he might be hungry." She told Red.

"That's fine, I was on my way to get him anyway, thank you." She told the nurse. "Ain't that right mommy's man." Red started with baby talk of her own.

The nurse left the room when she saw that Red was in a comfortable breast-feeding position. All Red was waiting for at this point, was for the doctor to sign her release papers.

She looked at her precious newborn with loving eyes.

"Boy, you look just like your daddy." It seemed every time she saw him, he favored Romero more and more.

After fifteen minutes of nursing, Red burped the baby and laid him back in his basinet. She tried to stay focused on reality, but her mind kept taking her back to the fantasy of her family being together. She wanted to forget Romero, but now that she had his miniature high yellow twin, that would be impossible.

Packing was proving to be a difficult task for her, so she would rest every few minutes to avoid any further complications.

She picked up her phone to be sure the nanny was in route to the hospital to pick up her and little RJ. She had actually already decided when she named him Romero that RJ would be his nickname. After sending the nanny a text message, Red noticed that she missed a call from Toni.

She returned the call and was immediately concerned when she heard sirens in Toni's background.

"Toni, what's going on?" Red asked her through the noise.

"We're on our way to Barnes Jewish." Toni was almost screaming because of the siren, but her frantic tone didn't help with the volume of her voice.

"We who? And what's happened?" Now Red was yelling. She almost woke the baby and decided to step in the hallway.

"Me and David. We were in an accident and David was shot. He's unconscious and I'm about to lose it. I tried calling Ivey, but she didn't answer. I even text her 911! If you hear from her, please tell her to return my call." Toni was nervous and afraid.

"Oh my God! Are you alright?" Asked a concerned Red.

"I feel like I'm about to lose my mind. I don't understand what's going on." Toni's comment confused Red more than she already was. "We're here, I'll call you back in a minute. And Red, please try to get in touch with Brandon and Ivey."

"Of course. And keep me posted." Red immediately hung up and called Ivey.

Just like Toni said, she didn't answer. In fact, her call went straight to
voicemail.

"Ivey, this is Red. Something is terribly wrong and you need to contact Toni as soon as humanly possible." Red said as she left the urgent message on Ivey's voicemail.

Red went back into the room to continue packing. She checked on RJ, but still couldn't shake what Toni had told her. It was like deja vu and she couldn't understand who would want to hurt David.

"Excuse me, Ms. Mason?" The nurse said interrupting her thoughts.
"You have a visitor."

"A visitor?" Red was perplexed.

The only visitors she had, had been Toni, David, Ivey, and Brandon, and since she knew full well that it couldn't be them, she prepared herself emotionally for the only other visitors she could think of, her parents, or at least one of them anyway. "That's fine." Red told the nurse as she turned to finish organizing her belongings.

She heard the door to her room open. She turned to greet her guest and she dropped the glass bottles in her hand, causing them to shatter and little RJ to be startled from his sleep. All the blood seemed to rush from her brain.

And then he spoke.

"Hello Red."

"Hello Romero."

## Ma Ma Mia

Today seemed like the longest day of her life. It was the first day Rocky had been to school since her mother's funeral. She managed to make it through thanks to the kush joint Quitta gave her to smoke before first period. So, by the time school was out, she was starving.

"I'm hungry as a hostage." Rocky said aloud as she walked home
from school.

Her little sisters were still traumatized from their mother's murder and had yet to return to school. It was so awkward for her to go straight home that she almost made a wrong turn to head to the twin's school. *Force of habit*, Rocky thought.

She headed home and all she could think about was food. When she stepped on the porch of the duplex she smelled the aroma of Mama Isa's plantains. Rocky went upstairs to see the twins already at the table ready to eat.

"Hola pretty girls." Rocky greeted the twins.

"Hi Kelly!" They replied not quite together sounding like a round. Mama Isa appeared from the kitchen like a phantom.

"Hola Mama." Rocky said only out of respect.

"There isn't enough for you." Mama Isa told Rocky.

"Enough?" Rocky had no idea what she was referring to. "La comida." She paused.

"So, you mean I can't eat here?" Rocky was flabbergasted.

"No hay suficiente dinero." Said Mama Isa.

"I can give you money Mama." Rocky said offering a solution to their dilemma.

Rocky figured that was it and Mama Isa's problem was solved. But
she continued to give Rocky a look that told her otherwise.

"Cual es el problema Mama?" Rocky asked in an effort to find out what the problem was.

"You have to go." Mama Isa said bluntly. "You will not corrupt these girls the way your mama did you. I don't want you around them, the way you are." She looked Rocky up and down with disgust.

"Please Mama Isa, I don't have anywhere to go!" Rocky begged.

She couldn't understand what was happening. Her world was being turned upside down.

"Go wherever you go until the middle of the night. I see you sneaking
in. Justo como su mama!" Her grandmother screamed.

She wasn't aware that Rocky had been hustling to help her provide for the girls.

"You don't care, you never have. You don't care about anyone that doesn't fit into your little box! You're probably glad my mama is dead, and you don't care if I live or die either!" By that point, Rocky was crying which caused the twins to be upset as well.

They got up from the table and rushed to Rocky's side. The girls held
on to her for dear life, afraid that if they let her go they would never see her again.

"Kelly please don't leave us!" Laniah cried.

"Can we go with you?" Asked Mariah.

"Laniah, I will never leave you, no matter where I am. I will come to check on you every day. And no Riah, you can't come with me, at least not now." She said looking up at Mama Isa through tears filled with hatred.

"You will never get them! Fuera!"

"I'm leaving, but I will be back." Rocky finally said to her as she went downstairs to pack as much of her belongings as she could carry.

The twins screamed her name when she walked out the door. It broke
her heart to have to leave them and it tortured her soul to hear
their cries and not be able to answer or console them.

She didn't have any relatives in St. Louis that she knew of, and even though she had a little bit of hustle money, she wasn't old enough to find a place of her own. So she went to the closest friend she had, Quitta.

Pinot Noir


It had been about eight hours since Ivey sent Quitta home with a note to meet with her mother after not being able to contact her over the phone. Afterward, she took a personal day and headed straight to the store for a bottle of wine. Ivey didn't even drink, but she needed to indulge. So, she figured red wine would be okay.

She sat on the floor in the comer of the living room. All she wanted was silence; no radio, no television, no telephone. She just wanted to be alone with her thoughts. Well, at least she thought she did, until she actually was.

What Quitta told her played in her mind like a bad rerun. Then thoughts of the man she was supposed to know, played as well. She was so confused at this point, she didn't know what to think.

She was three quarters way through the bottle and was now intoxicated. More so than she even realized, being a nondrinker. Brandon finally came home from work in the middle of her emotional may lay.

He saw Ivey's car outside, so he knew she was home. But when he walked in the house it looked abandoned. No lights were on, as well as, no radio or television, which was rare if she was home.

"Ivey!" Brandon called out to her.

The sound of his voice made her heart skip a beat and her stomach cringe all the same time. She had never been so emotionally confused in her life.

"Ivey!" Brandon yelled again.

He was 99% sure that she was at home and couldn't understand why she wouldn't answer him.

"I'm here." Ivey finally slurred sounding muffled and dry.

Brandon turned on the light in the living room as his eyes searched in the direction of her voice. When he saw her in the corner with a wine bottle he instantly became concerned.

"What's going on Ivey?" His voice was serious.

There was more silence as Ivey took a few more sips of wine. Brandon stood in the doorway patiently waiting for her to answer him.

"You tell me." She slurred once more.

"Well, from what I can tell, my wife is intoxicated in the dark. So, I'll ask again, what's going on?" Brandon asked again still remaining calm even though this situation was beginning to aggravate him.

"I hear things Brandon, very confusing and troubling things. And I
don't know how to feel about them." Ivey said vaguely.

"What things?" Now his aggravation was becoming apparent. "Ivey, what are you talking about?"

"LaQuitta Benton." She finally made her reveal.

"LaQuitta?" Brandon knew Quitta had the capacity to be a menace, but he couldn't understand what she had to do with the reason Ivey was drunk, on the floor, in the middle of the day.

"Yes LaQuitta, did you become a parrot since this morning?" The alcohol had caused her to speak more freely than normal.

Brandon walked over to Ivey and took the bottle of Pinot Nair from her. He held up the bottle to gage how much she had drank. He quickly retreated to the kitchen to get her a glass of water to assist in her sobriety.

"Here, drink this." He tried to give her the glass, but she waved him off.

"You drink it." She told him without even looking up at him.

"Ivey, I'm really trying to be patient and keep my cool. But it's becoming extremely difficult with you being rude and dismissive. Anyway, what does LaQuitta have to do with any of this?" Brandon asked not prepared for what he came home to.

Ivey tried to stand for the first time since she began drinking. She lost her balance and fell against the wall. Brandon instinctively ran to her side, but she snatched away from him.

"Let me go!" She screamed. "Did you try to force yourself on her?" Ivey caught Brandon off guard with her question.

The thought of Quitta's breakdown and the sub-sequential change in her behavior caused Brandon to immediately become suspicious as to the reason for all that was happening.

"Ivey, you know I wouldn't touch anyone but you. So, what are you talking about?" He spoke slowly and calmly.

"Well that's what I thought too until she came to my office and told
me what you did to her!" Emotions and alcohol clouded Ivey's judgment.

"Please come sit down so I can explain. And believe me when I tell
you, I didn't do anything to her. But I need you to listen." Brandon was very delicate about the situation considering the circumstances and Ivey's condition.

"Explain? You mean there's actually something to explain? Brandon I trusted you!" Ivey began to have an emotional breakdown.

Brandon felt he needed to get control of the situation.

"Ivey!" He yelled.

He frightened her; she had never heard him elevate his voice to that volume.

"I'm sorry, but you need to listen." He grabbed her shoulders and sat her on the couch.

She was still in a state of shock at the fact that he spoke to her in that tone. He crouched on the floor in front of her and held her hands.

"She approached me at the church Wednesday night. I gave her the portfolio and she hugged me, but the hug became completely inappropriate and I pushed her away. She initially implied that I wanted her, but when I told her how out of line she was, she broke down crying. But when you came in she transformed like an actress. The only reason I didn't say anything to you is because she promised it would never happen again. And she begged me not to say anything. Plus, baby you know me, I would never do anything to a child or any woman for that matter." Brandon looked deeply into Ivey's alcohol hazed eyes.

They were full of tears. She questioned her own judgment. Could she really believe that the man she fell in love with would betray her that way? Could a young girl be as conniving and manipulative as to tell a lie so destructive? Then she thought about a sixteen-year old Toni. Even in her inebriated state, Ivey could clearly see what she had missed all along. Brandon was not a sexual deviant and LaQuitta was emotionally inept.

"I believe you." She told him. "But I have a meeting with her mother tomorrow and it'll be your word against hers. I will definitely have to be removed from the situation due to conflict of interest." Ivey tried to reason like she wasn't tipsy.

Brandon kissed Ivey. He didn't care what tomorrow brought or what LaQuitta would say in this moment. He was just grateful to God that he had a true soul mate. And he knew now that no matter what, Ivey would have his back.

# ER

Waiting in the emergency room waiting area was excruciating, especially alone. Toni was more than happy when Ivey and Brandon finally showed up at the hospital. She had walked a hole in the linoleum as she waited to hear news about David's condition. So, it was a relief when Toni heard from her sister telling her that she was on the way to her side.

When they took David back to be examined, she was oblivious to his condition. She had no idea of his stability or the severity of what was going on with her fiancée.

"Antoinette Danes?" The male nurse called for Toni.

She almost jumped out of her skin at the sound of her own name.

"Yes, I'm here!" She rushed to the nurse.

"I'll take you back to Mr. James now." The nurse was very technical and uniform in his approach.

Toni followed him to the ER exam room that David was in. It seemed
like an eternity as they walked down the corridor that seemed like a gateway to either the dying or the sick. Either way, she wished she was somewhere else.

When she turned the corner of the room, Toni's knees buckled. The nurse managed to stop her from falling and helped her to David's side. The first sight of him made her sick to her stomach. His head was bandaged with white bandages and his arm was in a sling. He lay with his head propped up on a pillow and his eyes closed.

Toni felt sorry for him as she finally approached the bed and could clearly see swelling and bruising in David's face. He looked like he should have been in excruciating pain, but he was resting peacefully.

"Is he okay?" Toni whispered to the nurse as he typed on the hospital computer.

"The doctor will be in to speak with you soon. He's heavily medicated so he may be a little groggy." The nurse told her before exiting the room.

Toni pulled up a chair to the side of David's bed. Now the tables were turned, and she felt helpless. She also felt guilty that he was enduring this pain and suffering because of her tainted past. She buried her face in her hands and shed silent tears.

"Mrs. James?" The tall, tanned, green eyed doctor said as he entered the room.

Toni slowly raised her head as she attempted to wipe the tears away.

"I'm his fiancée, Ms. Danes." Toni said extending her hand. "How is he?" As tired as she was of being in the dark, she was actually afraid of what he might say.

"Well Ms. Danes, I'm Dr. Leschefske. I have to say, Mr. James is an extremely lucky man, and not for obvious reasons." The doctor said flirting, not so subtly. "It appears that his face hit the dashboard or the airbag, which caused him to have a mild concussion. And the bullet only grazed his left shoulder. We ran some tests and had to remove some fragments from his shoulder, other than that, he'll be fine. I just want to keep him overnight for observation." The doctor explained.

Toni gave a sigh of relief at the thought that his injuries were not life threatening and nowhere near as bad as they looked. But was it over? She thought as she looked down at this man that had been nothing but a blessing to her. But now, he's in a hospital bed because of her.

"Also ma'am, there are some officers here that would like to speak with you." The doctor said interrupting her self-pity.

He pointed her in the direction of the waiting area. She didn't know
what the police wanted to know, and she didn't have much to tell them. When she entered there were two uniformed officers; one white, one black.

"Hello Ms. Danes, I'm Sergeant Johnson and this is Lieutenant Ryan." The black officer said with his hand extended.

Toni reluctantly returned the gesture, but not without reservation.

"What's this about?" Toni asked the officers with suspicion. "I
already filed a report about the incident."

"Ma'am please, have a seat." Sergeant Johnson's tone was critical.

She sat as he suggested, but she couldn't shake the feeling that something was terribly wrong. After finding out that David's condition was stable, she was hoping things would start to look up. Toni sent a quick text to Ivey and asked her and Brandon to go in and sit with David.

"Ms. Danes, there has been a gentleman in a psychiatric rehab in Northwest Missouri for about a year. Originally, he was being treated for severe third-degree bums. But after he started to heal physically, he seemed to check out mentally. He wouldn't talk or communicate, so the doctors classified him as psychotic. It wasn't until after he escaped from rehab and the staff searched his room, that we realized exactly how psychotic he is." The officer handed Toni a shoe box.

The contents of the box almost made Toni vomit. She held her mouth in horror as her eyes jetted to each item causing her even more terror.

There were pictures of her, beaten and tied to a bed. She was conscious on a few of them, just barely. There was a pair of her underwear and several letters detailing her kidnapping and assault, along with papers that had *DIE BITCH* scribbled all over them. The last straw was the images of her assailants, including Coco and Peaches.

Toni began to have flashes of the time she spent confined and abused. She dropped the box on the floor and moved away from the officers. She felt confused and violated.

"Wha . . . what is this?" She asked not understanding why the officers would refresh this memory.

Then what they told her started to register.

"Escaped, who escaped? What are you talking about?" Toni asked.

"Does the name Troy Brown ring a bell?" The officer asked.

Her body went numb. One thing she remembered very clearly about her assault is that Troy was the ring leader, beside Peaches. He told everyone what to do and when.

"He's dead." Toni said like the wind had been knocked out of her.

"Honestly, he should be. He was the only survivor in the explosion at
his home last year, and he wasn't expected to live this long. We've kept an eye on his storage unit and surviving family to see if we could get a lead on a suspect. So, when we got word that someone went to the unit and got a description on the vehicle and plate number, we knew he made it back to St. Louis. And now we know why.

"Okay, so go arrest him!" Toni knew she wouldn't feel safe until he was dead or in jail.

"It's not quite that easy Ms. Danes, we don't know where he is at the moment. But we're prepared to have an officer escort you until he's apprehended." He said.

Just the thought of being afraid and helpless infuriated Toni.

"I don't need protection; I need a peace of mind!" Toni was frustrated and beginning to feel like 'old' Toni.

All she knew, is that if she found him first, she wouldn't be the one that needs protecting.

True Colors


Rocky felt like a hobo walking the streets of Jennings with her bags. She had tried to contact Quitta for several hours with no luck. Her last resort was to just show up. Even though she hated pop ups, Rocky felt she didn't have much of a choice.

As she knocked on the door, she silently prayed that Gwen would not be the one to answer. She waited anxiously as she heard footsteps coming closer to the door by the second. Her prayers were answered when she saw Quitta peek her head through the curtains. Quitta quickly stepped out on the porch.

"Girl, this is not the best time." Quitta said immediately.

Then she looked at Rocky and noticed her face and her luggage. She appeared to have been crying, a lot.

"What's goin' on Rock?" Quitta questioned.

"I need somewhere to stay for a little while." Rocky looked down at the porch. "Mama Isa put me out cause I'm gay."

Quitta gasped.

"What, you mean you're gay?" They both erupted into laughter.

Quitta could see that the situation was grim and wanted to lighten the
mood.

"It's some pretty heavy shit goin' on around here too, but go to the
basement door and wait; grab Shadow if you see her." Quitta instructed.

Rocky obeyed orders as she struggled to pull her bags down the basement steps. After about five minutes of waiting, Quitta finally made it to the door. She motioned for Rocky to keep quiet and follow her. They maneuvered through boxes and clothes until they finally made it to the door to the upstairs.

Quitta took a deep breath. "Stay close." She whispered to Rocky.

They hurriedly shuffled through the dining room and into the Quitta's bedroom without being noticed by Gwen. Once they made it successfully, they both gave sighs of relief.

"You cool?" Quitta asked as she helped Rocky situate her belongings.

"I'll be okay. What's goin' on around here?" Rocky was relieved she had something to momentarily take her mind off her own situation.

"That perv put his hands on me." Quitta said very non-chalantly.

"What perv?" Rocky was confused at this point.

"Brandon." Quitta rattled off like it meant nothing.

"Quitta, what are you talking about? Are we talking about the same Brandon that was 'your man' a week ago, the same Brandon that's married to Mrs. Cameron?" Rocky had become suspicious.

"Yeah, and, whatchu tryna say?" Quitta said defensively.

Rocky had to think very carefully about what she would say next. "I'm saying, this it some serious shit." She needed Quitta's help and didn't want to rub her the wrong way with accusations, so she kept her real opinion to herself. "So, you told your mom?"

"Nope, Mrs. Cameron did." Quitta said as she flopped down on her queen-sized bed.

"You told Mrs. Cameron?" Rocky was outdone, but she continued to contain her judgment.

"Yeah, I figured she needed to know what kinda man she's dealing with." Quitta said matter of factly.

She also seemed very untouched by everything. To Rocky, she didn't seem traumatized in the least little bit. But she kept those opinions to herself as well, although she wanted to know how far Quitta planned to go with this.

"So, are you pressing charges?" Rocky asked in an effort to make her
friend see just how serious her accusations were.

"My mom said we are, but it seemed like more of a threat to me than anything else. Either way, he has to pay." Quitta was now flicking television channels with her remote.

It bothered Rocky that she seemed so unconcerned about how this could affect other people's lives.

"Did he hurt you Quitta?" Rocky found herself asking.

Quitta continued to flip through the stations without responding. Finally, she spoke.

"I don't wanna talk about this anymore."

She continued to watch TV seemingly unfazed by the situation at hand. And Rocky was not in a position to speak on the way she felt at that moment, so she remained silent.

At that second, Rocky realized the depths of Quitta's deception, and she wanted no parts of it. As soon as she got enough money together, she would leave Quitta to her own devices. The game she played was dangerous for all parties involved. But something told Rocky that Quitta was not who she thought she was and didn't care whose lives she ruined.

2a.m.

Rocky slept on the floor next to Quitta's bed, closest to the wall so she wouldn't be spotted by Gwen if she came in the room. Her bladder had awakened her from her sleep and Quitta was in a coma. She tried to awaken her several times, but had no luck.

She danced around for a few minutes then decided she couldn't hold it any longer. Rocky quietly crept through the hallway until she found the bathroom. After relieving herself, she returned to her sanity and immediately got nervous. She ran back to the safety of Quitta's room and closed the door.

"Where you go?" Quitta said almost scaring Rocky back to the bathroom.

"Girl, you gone give me a heart attack! I went to the bathroom. I tried to wake you up." Rocky explained.

When she looked at Quitta, she was pointing in the direction of what Rocky thought was a closet, with her eyes still closed. Rocky walked over and opened the door to a half bath with a private shower.

"It would've been nice if you had told me that BEFORE I almost got us busted."

But when she turned around, Quitta had already drifted back to sleep.

"Forget you." Rocky said as she tried to find a comfortable position on the floor.

Rocky laid on her back staring up at the ceiling, hoping sleep would come back to her. It took forever for her to fall asleep originally, with thoughts of her mother and the sounds of her little sister's cries in her head.

She turned on her side to search for a more comfortable position when she noticed a pink notebook underneath Quitta's bed. Rocky peeked over the bed at Quitta to be sure she was still asleep. The notebook was just in arms reach as she pulled it toward her.

*My Diary,* was written in rainbow ink on the front cover. Rocky was apprehensive about continuing at first, but she needed to know what was going on in Quitta's head. She turned to Quitta's most recent entry.

*Dear Diary,*
*My plan seems to be coming together nicely. Well at least plan B. I refuse to be ignored or rejected by anyone, even him! I can't believe he thought he would get away with treating me like that. If I can't have him, he will never be happy, especially not with that perfect, goody two shoes, Ivey. Maybe next time I'll cry rape, that'll teach him!!! I'll save that for plan C.*

Rocky flipped through the pages of the demented schemes and plots thought and carried out by the hands of an obsessed sixteen-year-old girl that clearly needed help. She put the diary back in its place and tried to figure out what to do next. Should she reveal what she knows and stop Quitta from destroying Brandon and Ivey's lives? Or does she remain loyal to her friend and pretend she never saw a word. She wished now she would've never opened that diary.

## Strange Days

The butterflies in Ivey's stomach were working overtime. She was certain the wine she had the night before was the culprit. Plus, with everything else that was going on with Quitta, David and Toni, she didn't know if she was coming or going.

As she sat behind her desk, Ivey looked over the report that held the accusations against her husband. She didn't believe a word of it. But the kind of person Ivey was, wouldn't allow her to comprehend how someone could tell this kind of lie with no regard for who she's hurting. Ivey couldn't understand, but she planned to be prepared.

Ivey prayed, and she already had an attorney on standby just in case LaQuitta continued with her debauchery of Brandon's character; one of the best in the city to be exact, Attorney Jillian Lee. She and Brandon already consulted with her regarding the matter, and she instructed them to stick with the truth and remain calm and confident.

LaQuitta and her mother were already fifteen minutes late and Ivey was getting anxious. She was already nauseous and had a headache from her prior day's activities, so the need to get this over with as soon as possible was pertinent.

"Mrs. Cameron?" Ivey's secretary said upon her entrance.

All Ivey could think was, *about time.*

"Yes Pam."

"Mrs. Benton called, she said she needs to reschedule; something about her car." She told Ivey.

This only infuriated Ivey and caused her even more anxiety.

"Did she say when?" Ivey asked.

"No Ma'am, she said she'd call back later today." Pam explained. Ivey sighed.

"Okay fine. I don't feel well, so I'm leaving for the day.

"When she calls, schedule her at her earliest convenience and if you have to cancel whatever is on my schedule at that time, then so be it. Oh, and be sure to cc the principal and the superintendent please." Ivey ordered.

Yes ma'am, will do Mrs. Cameron." Pam stood in the doorway absorbing the information like a computer.

Pam was a nineteen-year-old college student. And although she always wore her hair pulled back and round, wire framed glasses, Ivey could tell she was attractive, but just didn't know it yet. Her petite five-foot four frame, was shapely, but was usually covered with frumpy clothing. She had a flawless caramel complexion that if she ever dared to wear makeup, she wouldn't even need any.

"Thank you. And Pam?" Ivey said before Pam walked out of the office.

"Yes ma'am?"

"For the last time, call me Ivey."


*Afterschool*

After not seeing Quitta or Mrs. Cameron in school, Rocky became concerned. She managed to get out of the house that morning without running into Gwen, but she wasn't so sure how she would get back in.

As she got closer to Quitta's and contemplated how this would all play out, she noticed that a familiar car had been following her. When she jogged her memory, she almost became violently ill when she realized it was the same Cadillac Seville that Smiley, (or Slimey as she would prefer to call him) the man who murdered her mother drove.

Her heart began to pound, and she felt light headed. Then she instinctively felt around inside her back pack to make sure her protection was in place. She couldn't imagine why he would be following her, but she planned to be prepared for whatever.

The black Seville crept up slowly from behind her. Rocky pretended not to recognize the vehicle and continued on as if she wasn't shaking from the inside out. For a few seconds, everything seemed to go silent and slow down. She could hear the thump of her heartbeat pounding in her ears.

Then she saw it. She saw the face of the man that murdered her mother. To her, he had the face of the devil; a face she would never forget. As he drove past slowly, he motioned to her with his finger. He pointed to her, and Rocky felt it meant he was coming for her. She continued to ignore him as he went by. Finally, Rocky gave a sigh of relief. She felt like she hadn't taken a breath at all, until now.

Her apprehension about showing up at Quitta's was nothing compared to the emotional roller coaster she had just experienced. As she approached the house, she was actually relieved to even possibly be able to get off the street.

When she knocked, Rocky prepared herself to come face to face with Gwen. But to her surprise and relief, Quitta answered the door and let her in.

"What happened to you today?" Rocky asked as she stole a French fry from Quitta's plate.

"Well, we were on our way to the school, but I'm assuming one of them crazy niggas my momma deal with, slashed all four of her tires. So needless to say, she's pissed and of course it's my fault." Quitta said like it was common for her to take the blame for things she hadn't done. "But it really don't make sense, cause she don't bring nobody home, so I don't know who it could be." Quitta said, but she really didn't care.

"So where she at?" Rocky asked.

"At the shop, tryna make sure the tires was the only thing that got tampered with." Quitta said rolling her eyes at the whole situation.

"Can I get something to eat, damn?" Rocky said after watching Quitta demolish her plate of fries.

"My bad, I'll fix you something." Quitta offered.

Rocky surfed the TV channels and eagerly awaited some sustenance. She had almost dozed off when she heard a blood curdling scream. Rocky grabbed her back pack and ran to the kitchen. She had one hand inside her bag when she entered the kitchen and saw Quitta holding a bloody ball of fur and a note.

"What is it?" Rocky asked frantically.

"It's Shadow!!!" Quitta screamed as she fell to her knees and the note drifted to the floor.

Rocky retrieved the blood-stained note and read it.

*You can run but you can't hide! Checkmate!*
*I'll be in touch if you come to your senses,*
*before it is too late.*

## Q and A

"Where have you been?" Red questioned Romero as he carried her luggage inside the house.

"Baby, let's get you settled, and I told you we will sit down and I will
explain everything." Rome said.

After they held each other for about fifteen minutes at the hospital, and rode home in silence, Red needed some answers.

"Do you have any idea what I've been through without you?" Red questioned rhetorically.

"Red, take the baby upstairs, and I'll be there when I'm finished." He pointed her in the direction of the stairs.

She reluctantly obeyed, but she was eager for answers. Red stood in
the large window in the rear hallway to observe Raina and Ryan playing in the backyard. They seemed so happy with no worries to boggle down their hearts and minds.

117

RJ squirmed in her arms and searched for a nipple. She almost opened the door to Peaches' room, but quickly changed her mind. Preparing to breast feed, Red loosened her top on the way to her room. Just as she sat on the bed, Romero entered.

He was even finer than she remembered; six foot five, dark caramel and handsome with deep set, dark eyes and a chiseled chin. It appeared that he was in top physical condition as well, but that did not deter her from wanting her answers.

Romero pulled the ottoman up to Red's feet and sat, placing her feet in his lap. He gently massaged her foot and kissed her big toe. Then he looked at her with his son, taking them all in as if he were absorbing their life force. She watched his every move. He seemed different somehow. Red couldn't quite put her finger on what it was, but he had definitely never kissed her feet before.

"Ask away." Romero said giving her permission to bombard him with questions.

"Where-have-you-been?" Red asked slowly and deliberately due to having to repeat herself.

"I miss you." Romero said looking into her eyes.

"Do you know what I've been through thinking you were dead? Wondering what I would tell our son about his father?" Red continued with her interrogation.

"I never stopped thinking about you." He spoke like he couldn't hear what she was saying.

"Romero!" Red raised her voice startling the baby momentarily.

Romero took a deep breath and prepared to tell Red everything she wanted to know.

### After the shooting

*Romero was unconscious for less than a minute before he awoke to the sounds of sirens getting closer to Peaches' house. He was weak and in pain, but he mustered up enough energy to pull the car away from the house and exit the vehicle.*

*He was losing blood quickly and he knew he needed medical attention. Romero immediately dialed the number of Kimball Michaels, a former med student that was on call whenever Rome had an emergency.*

*After giving Kimball his location the next twenty-four hours were hazy; Rome could remember being carried out of the bushes, then carried into a house, and then a painful bullet extraction. Kimball was even amazed that Romero made it through everything alive.*

*As soon as he was well enough, Romero left the country. Even though he was very thorough about fingerprints and being seen, he had to be sure the police hadn't tied him to the eight murders he thought he'd committed. It wasn't until he was in Argentina for a month and having his people keep an eye on Red, that he was informed that Peaches was still alive. Then, when he found out that Red hadn't aborted his baby, he knew there was still a chance that he could one day be in the baby's life and she couldn't hate him completely.*

*The money he acquired in the game allowed him to live very comfortably in Argentina. In fact, he even procured a small business and was able to go legit.*

*His profession was not the only thing different about Romero. He even gained a great deal of spiritual wisdom. He wasn't sure when or how it happened, but he felt remorseful about the murders he'd committed and the drugs he'd sold. Romero had developed a conscious.*

*He often thought back to Jojo and he truly missed his brother. He wished he was there to share in the knowledge that Romero now possessed. He also prayed for forgiveness and hoped Red would forgive him for all he did to her and Peaches.*

*But in his gaining of knowledge, he also knew that everything happened for a reason, and he would not be where he was spiritually if not for all that happened.*

*While he was away, he evaluated every aspect of his life; the money and drugs, even his mother and brother Rio. But he felt the worst about being a catalyst to Toni's destruction. He felt he could have been a much better influence, considering the age difference. He also kept watch over her and was happy to know that David was in her life and making a difference.*

*Romero told Red about everything that happened in that last year that he could remember. Red told him about her newly found relationship with Toni. And they reminisced about their life before the tragedy.*

"Is there anything else you want to know?" Rome asked.

"Why didn't you try to contact me before now?" Red needed to know.

"I was afraid you hated me. It wasn't until the Creator gave me the
courage to face my true demons, that I was able to face you. And I had to see my son." He told her from his heart.

The baby was sound asleep, and Red looked down at her son, then back at his father.

"Please don't leave us again." Red said with tears in her eyes.

"I love you." She had never heard him say those words to her.

Red parted her lips to speak. Before she could say a word, Peaches' nurse rushed into her room.

"Ms. Mason! Your sister is crashing! I just want to verity the DNR in her file." She said with urgency.

The few seconds of silence seemed like minutes.

"If she's going . . . let her go, the Do Not Resuscitate order stands."

## The Meeting

It took Gwen all of a day to make sure her car was running properly, and then file a police report and restraining order against Clarence. But she was unable to provide them with an address, so it was basically a matter of procedure.

She couldn't believe that after how careful she was, he was still able to find out where she lived. *Stalker,* she thought. But the only reason she knew the ways to stay under the radar, is because of her tendency to be a bit 'stalkerish' herself in the past. But she shook off that thought as she got ready for her meeting with the infamous Mrs. Cameron.

Gwen knew that Quitta had taken a liking to Ivey, so she was already envious of her to start. But seeing now that Quitta turned her sights on destroying Ivey's husband, she was almost happy to oblige Quitta with the lie Gwen knew she was telling.

"We're leaving in two minutes!" Gwen yelled through the house to Quitta.

Gwen tried to dress as professional as possible wearing a Donna Karen pant suit. She even threw on a fake pair of reading glasses for effect.

Quitta had been dressed for about twenty minutes. She was schooling Rocky on how to get back in through the basement without being noticed. They already planned for Rocky to leave the house after Gwen and Quitta left for the meeting at the school.

"Quitta!" She heard her mother scream. "C'mon!"

Quitta turned to Rocky to reiterate her instructions.

"Remember, wait till we get off the block." Quitta said.

"Aight damn, I ain't retarded." Rocky retorted.

Just as planned, Quitta and Gwen left for the school and Rocky left the house as soon as the coast was clear. When Rocky reached the end of the block, her blood boiled when she saw the old black Seville again. But this time he stopped.

"You lookin' for some work baby girl?" His voice made her skin
crawl.

"You lookin' for a mutha fuckin cemetery?" Rocky barked without
breaking her stride.

"Youngsta." He said as he laughed when he drove away.

Rocky made a few decisions that day, and at the top of that list was her promise that if she ever carne face to face with 'Slimey' again, she would make him sorry he ever saw her face.

Ivey's office

Gwen, Quitta, and Ivey all sat quietly awaiting Mrs. Jarvis, the Principal, and Mr. Farlin, the Superintendent's arrival. Ivey was given strict instructions by her attorney not to discuss the matter without a third-party present.

Mrs. Jarvis and Mr. Farlin entered the office together. Ivey stood to greet them and shake their hands, as did Gwen. Quitta however, continued to sit with her arms folded across her chest.

"Have some manners!" Gwen spat at Quitta.

"Hello." She said without moving a muscle.

Mrs. Jarvis began the conversation without hesitation.

"We just want to be clear about the accusations against Mrs. Cameron's husband, Brandon Cameron. So you allege that he tried to force himself on you, is that correct?" The Principal questioned Quitta.

Quitta took a deep breath and sighed like she was tired of repeating herself.

"Like I said, he started rubbing on me and he tried to kiss me. Then when I tried to resist he grabbed me, and that's when Mrs. Cameron came in. He was talking about I owe him for putting my portfolio together." She lied like she was reading a script.

Both Mrs. Jarvis and Mr. Farlin had known Brandon for several years, so they knew that the likelihood of what she was saying being true, was slim to none. So, it truly pained them to have to make an executive decision regarding Ivey, despite their gut feelings.

"Well unfortunately, due to the nature of these accusations, we have to ask you to step down until the investigation is complete." Mr. Farlin educated Ivey.

"Step down? You mean to a different position?" Ivey was now concerned about her reputation and livelihood.

"No Mrs. Cameron, we have to suspend you . . . with pay for now. But we have to either substantiate or dismiss this claim before we make any further decisions regarding your employment." Mr. Farlin told her reluctantly.

The work Ivey had done as the head counselor was remarkable. She created programs that truly made a difference in the student's lives. He knew that Ivey actually cared about them and he would hate to lose her.

Ivey however, felt like she could literally throw-up when she heard the outcome of her fate. She thought for sure she would have to be replaced as Quitta's counselor; she had no idea they would ask her to leave altogether.

"We will be in touch with everyone about the investigation process.

125

Because the alleged incident took place elsewhere, our only involvement has to deal with the fact that you are related to the accused Mrs. Cameron." The Superintendent continued.

Everyone except Ivey stood to leave. She wanted to pack some things to take home, plus she needed to marinate on what she had just heard. She began to become emotional, but she knew that would only give Satan power and control over the situation. Ivey decided to put that energy into trusting God and praying for the best.

She began packing personal pictures of her and Brandon, as well as, a picture of her mother and her college certificate. While Ivey filled her box with the things most important to her, she was startled by a presence in the doorway.

"Raquel, you frightened me. Come in, what can I do for you?" Ivey tried not to sound the way she felt."

"Are you leaving, Mrs. Cameron?" Rocky asked surprised to see Ivey
packing.

"I'm afraid so Raquel. It'll only be temporary." Ivey said prayerfully.

"Does this have something to do with Quitta?" Rocky asked.

"I'm sorry, but you know I can't discuss that situation with you. And I'm sure you probably already know more than you should." Ivey told her.

Rocky pondered over the decisions she made earlier that day. To her, they were more than decisions, they were promises.

"I'm leaving too Mrs. Cameron." Rocky said out of the blue.

"Leaving, where are you going?" Ivey asked with a look of concern.

"It's too much on my grandmother to take care of all of us so I'm going to stay with some relatives for a little while." Rocky lied.

"Please call me if you need anything." Ivey said giving Rocky a business card. "Anything." She reiterated looking into Rocky's eyes.

"Thank you, Mrs. Cameron, you've always been here for me and I
appreciate that." Rocky said, sad that she would miss Ivey. "But before I
go, I wanted to give you something." Rocky dug around in her backpack. "I hope this will help you and your husband." Rocky said as she handed Ivey the pink notebook with rainbow writing on the front cover.

Ivey flipped through the pages and was utterly amazed and appalled at the things she saw. She couldn't believe the complexity of a mind so young. She also couldn't believe Rocky would betray her friend to help her, but she was grateful; it could only be God, she thought.

Rocky turned to walk out of the office.

"Rocky . . . thank you." Ivey said with tears starting to form in her
eyes.

As Rocky opened the door to leave, she turned back to look at Ivey.

"No Ivey, thank you."

Main Course




Randy invited the family over for dinner to make an announcement. He had to tell the family something "extremely important", as he so eloquently put it.

David was home from the hospital and feeling 100% better. He stayed with Toni for a few days, so he wouldn't have far to walk to get to the things he needed, and so she could take care of him.

The same situation that Toni thought would push David away, actually made their bond stronger. The three days they spent together were beautiful. The only problem they did encounter was the urge to give in to their impulses. Their sexual tension was off the charts.

With the wedding only two weeks away, they were having a very difficult time staying focused. So, as soon as he was better, David immediately returned to sleeping in his own abode. He needed to stay strong in his conviction to not have sex with Toni before they got married, but being around her day and night made it almost impossible.

Ivey and Brandon were happy to get away from all the confusion going on in their lives. So dinner at Dad's was actually a welcomed gesture, especially since she was still feeling down about work.

The whole situation was beginning to effect more than Ivey's yearning to be around and help her students, she was feeling physically and emotionally drained as well. And Brandon, as usual, was there for her and he always kept a positive head. His constant good mood despite all that was going on was beginning to annoy her.

Both couples pulled up to Randy's house at almost the same time. Randy stood in the doorway and smiled at the choices in men his daughters made, as he watched both Brandon and David open the car doors for his girls. An emotional knot formed in his throat at the thought of what he had to tell his family.

"Hello, my beauties!" Randy greeted them with hugs.

He followed up with manly hugs and firm handshakes with David and Brandon.

"You ready to tie that knot?" Randy asked David.

"Yes sir, I wish we could do it today." David told Randy, looking into Toni's eyes.

The couples followed Randy inside the house and into the dining room. The table was beautifully set, and the aroma of Regina's cooking made everyone's mouth water.

"Mmmm, it smells good in here." Brandon said rubbing his stomach.

"I second that emotion!" David added.

"Well I hope everyone enjoys." Regina said as she entered the room with the first course of homemade chicken noodle soup and caesar salad.

Randy stood in the doorway watching his family; the family he never thought he would see together in his home. It saddened him to think of the possibility of this all coming to an end due to what he was about to reveal to them.

While they broke bread with one another, everyone laughed and joked as they enjoyed Regina's fabulous chicken marsala. Everyone seemed to forget all the confusion happening in their lives. They were happy. They were a family.

The dinner was topped off with caramel cake for dessert. Everyone was stuffed to the gills and Randy felt it was time to make his announcement. He tapped his fork to his glass to get everyone's attention.

"As you all know, I brought us all together today because I have something I need to tell you." He placed sealed envelopes in front of Ivey and Toni. "The contents of those envelopes are going to change everyone's lives. But I need you two to understand that if I would've known sooner, so would you." He told them as they gave each other puzzled looks.

He gave them a nod indicating it was okay to open the envelopes. Their reactions were totally different, but equally as disturbing to Randy. Toni held her mouth in utter disbelief as tears ran down her face. And Ivey just simply threw up all over the floor.

"I would have told you if I knew before now, I promise!" Randy cried.

*The Phone Call*
*(two weeks ago)*

*"Hello, may I speak with Rufus please." Randy said into the phone as he waved goodbye to Toni.*

*Brenda and her attitude were on the other end.*

*"Who is this?" She asked screening Rufus's phone call.*

*"It's Randy, Brenda." He said with reservation.*

*"Randy, what the hell you want with Rufus?" Brenda asked with
suspicion.*

*"Honestly, I could talk to either of you. I was calling about Red. Ivey and Toni seem to think that neither of you plan to donate blood to help with her recovery. You all are aware that she is in desperate need of a blood donor, aren't you?" Randy hoped that there was something he could say that would make a difference.*

*"Yeah, I heard. But I'm in need of some monetary donation. Can I get some help with that?" Brenda said without an ounce of sarcasm or empathy.*

*"Let me speak to Rufus please. Maybe he actually cares about what
happens to his daughter." Randy started to become agitated with Brenda.*

*Brenda began laughing uncontrollably.*

*"Peaches is already gone, so what difference does that make?" She asked, but Randy could tell she was being sarcastic.*

*"Brenda, I'm talking about Red!" He said like she had missed the point.*

*"I know who the fuck you talkin' about nigga, I ain't stupid! The question is, do you know?"*

*Randy was tired of the game Brenda was playing.*

*"What are you talking about?" Randy yelled into the phone.*

*"Wow, I figured your ass would try to push the shit to the back of your mind out of guilt, but damn! Lois is dead and gone, and you still don't wanna admit what happened." Brenda said like she was tired of him pretending.*

*Just at that moment, Randy remembered a drunken night at one of his and Lois's New Year's Eve parties, over twenty years ago. He could barely remember the details of the night after it happened. But the fact that he tried his hardest to erase the memory from his mind, made the night even less memorable.*

*"What does that have to do with this?" Randy asked.*

*Brenda exhaled a breath into the phone like she was sick of everything.*

*"Rufus ain't Red's daddy you ass, . . .you are!"*

"After talking to Brenda everything became so confusing, but I had to know the truth. So I went to the hospital to see if I was a match for her. When it turned out I was a match, I felt my first duty as her father was to donate blood and make sure she was going to be okay." Randy told them.

"What about the truth about you cheating on momma?" Ivey interrupted.

Randy could see that Ivey was more hurt by this situation than he expected. Toni was in shock, but her reaction displayed more surprise than Ivey's disappointment.

"That was a long time ago Ivey. You weren't even born yet. Your mother and I were young, and I admit I made some mistakes, we both did. I'm so sorry sweetheart." Randy pleaded.

After cleaning up her mess, Ivey stood up and started collecting her
things and Brandon followed suit.

"I spent all these years tryna convince Toni to give you a chance, but you deserved her treatment all along!" Ivey said furiously.

She stormed out of the house and all Brandon could do was try to be a
buffer in the situation. He had never seen her so upset before.

"Okay everyone, have a good evening. Regina, the food was wonderful. Bye Dad. Alright Toni, David call me." Brandon said to everyone on his way out the door.

Toni, on the other hand, still sat quietly at the dining room table. She was numb and wasn't sure how to feel. She had been upset with her dad for so long, that this didn't seem like enough to revert back to her past hatred. Plus, if she could be forgiven, it was only her duty to forgive her father for something he did so long ago.

Everyone sat in silence for a few minutes. Then Toni finally spoke.

"I'm going to call my sister." Toni said before exiting the room.

"Please tell Ivey I'm truly sorry for this." Randy begged.

Toni stopped at the door and turned to look at her father.

"I'm not talking about Ivey; I'm calling Red."

## Emotional Breakdown

After storming out of her father's house, Ivey sat in silence as Brandon drove them home. He tried to engage her in small talk, but she wouldn't bite. It was clear to him that she was beyond upset and he had never seen her so angry before, nor did he ever want to again.

Even after they got home Ivey continued with the silent treatment. Brandon couldn't understand why she had blown the situation out of proportion, but the last thing he wanted to do was be insensitive and offend her any further.

"You hungry?" He asked trying to get some inkling of conversation from her.

"Absolutely not. This whole situation has made me sick to my stomach." She said as she plopped down on the couch.

Ivey thought about the events of the past few days. Despite everything else that was going on, she was at least relieved about what the attorney told them about Quitta's diary. Because it was still in investigation stage and no criminal charges had been filed, Ms. Lee was confident that the diary would be enough to get Quitta to admit the lie and get some help. But that made Ivey understand the reason behind Quitta's intentions even less.

Then she thought about David and Toni, and the fact that the one good thing that came out of her visit to her father's, was seeing that he was okay and fully recovered. Toni hadn't spoken much about the incident, except for the fact that the culprit was Troy Brown. In fact, she seemed to not want to discuss the matter at all. The only thing she would say is, "I'll deal with it when the time comes." And she'd leave it at that.

"Ivey, did you hear me?" Brandon asked breaking her concentration.

"What?"

"I said, I understand it's a shock, but I'm just curious as to why you're so upset about this thing with your dad." He inquired.

Ivey sat up tall in her seat, and it was clear that her irritation level had
elevated to ten with his comment.

"Are you serious? So, you think it's okay that he cheated on my mom with that skank down the street, after she 'pretended' they were friends? Or is it okay that I have a sister that wasn't in my life the way she should've been because of his infidelity?" She ranted.

The questions were completely rhetorical, and Brandon knew better than to answer.

137

"Baby, I understand all of that, what I'm saying is, you've had time to forgive him for leaving when he divorced your mom. And you forgave him when he left you with your grandma after your mom died. So, I'm just trying to understand why this is so unforgiveable." Brandon tried to comprehend.

"So how would you feel if you found out you had a brother your age because your dad cheated on your mom?" Ivey felt she had made a valid point.

"I'd be furious, but my parents are still together. Look, I can see you being a little upset, but I think you're being too hard on him." Brandon tried to reason.

"We're talking about somebody's life Brandon. That girl doesn't even know who she is! Then to think how her life had to be anytime her own mother didn't care if she lived or died! She shouldn't have had to live like that; no child should!" By this point Ivey was in an uproar.

"Ivey, calm down babe. All I'm saying is, we're children of God and we teach forgiveness to everyone we come in contact with. We can't be hypocrites. So, be mad. Have your moment. But you've got to forgive him and move on. You said some really hurtful things to him. That happened over twenty years ago, and you can't persecute him; I'm sure God isn't." Brandon said knowing he needed to make Ivey revert back to her spirit.

She sat quietly without responding at first. She knew Brandon was absolutely right, but Ivey was harboring more than resentment for her father; she had a secret. And that alone was causing her more turmoil that everything else she was dealing with all together.

Ivey opened her mouth to speak.

"Brandon, I . . ." She stopped.

"What is it baby? Talk to me." Brandon pleaded.

"I'm pregnant."

Family Ties


Toni barely had the car door closed before Red's phone began to ring in her ear. David wasn't sure what she was planning, but he was going along for the ride. When the voicemail picked up, Toni was about to leave a message. Then she realized there was nothing about this situation that should be left on a voicemail, she needed to talk to Red in person.

She sped down I-64 west thinking of what exactly she planned to say to Red. Her mind was moving as fast as her sports car.

"Baby, are you okay? You haven't said a word since we left your
dad's." David was concerned about her state of mind.

"It's so surreal David. I don't really know what to say to her. I'm praying that God guides my tongue when we get to her house." She said realizing how at a loss for words she really was.

"You'll be okay. And I'll be with you every step of the way."
He assured her.

Her mind was eased momentarily, but the closer she got
to Red's, her anxiety grew again. What would Red say? Would she
blame Randy for abandoning her? Or would she even accept them
as her family at all?

Toni never thought she would care so much about another
person's feelings, especially not Red's. There was a time when she
wouldn't care about this situation one way or the other. But now
she felt everything in her life had purpose and God wouldn't
reveal this to her if she wasn't supposed to act on it.

A black limousine with a local funeral home logo pulled
away from Red's home as Toni and David pulled into the
driveway. They gave one another puzzled looks as if to speak
without speaking. As they approached the door, Toni noticed a
car she recognized as a rental in the driveway. She really hoped
she wasn't intruding, but she felt this was more than worth the
intrusion.

When Toni rang the bell, a short stout Mexican woman
answered the
door.

"May I help you please?" The woman said with a Spanish
accent.

"Is Drea Mason home?" Toni asked not sure which name
she should use.

"Si, who should I tell her is here?" The woman asked.

"Toni and David." Toni replied.

141

The woman left them standing outside the door for so long, Toni began to become concerned. She knocked on the door this time instead of ringing the bell. Seconds later, Red opened the door in haste.

"I'm sorry for leaving you two out here so long, come in." Red said letting them inside and leading them to her office. "I've actually been meaning to call you, but so much is going on." They entered the office and sat across the desk from one another. "So to what do I owe this visit?" Red asked.

"You first, you said you were gonna call me?" Toni reminded her.

"Toni, a LOT has happened since I saw you at the hospital last." Red
paused and looked down before continuing. "Peaches passed away the day me and the baby came home." Red revealed.

Toni wasn't expecting to hear something so tragic and wasn't sure how she felt. She hated to hear about anyone losing their lives; but this was the same woman that tried to take hers. But despite the past, Toni had dedicated her life to God and change, and she prayed for mercy on Peaches' soul. The most important thing Toni learned in her growth was forgiveness.

"I'm so sorry to hear that Red. How are the kids taking it?" Toni asked sincerely concerned about Raina and Ryan.

"Thank you, they're some little soldiers. They've actually helped
me to stay strong through all of this." Red admitted. "Honestly, I didn't think you would be interested in knowing. I apologize for being presumptuous." She said.

142

Now Toni was apprehensive about whether or not now was the right time to give Red news of this magnitude.

"So, what did you come all the way out here for?" Red said as if she
was reading Toni's mind.

David and Toni gave each other momentary eye contact, but David was not in a position to help her with this. She needed to do what she had to do.

"Well . . . I know who donated the blood that saved your life." Toni blurted out.

There was a moment of silence before the office door swung open.

"Babe, RJ's crying, I think he needs to be fed."

"Rome?" Toni stood in shock with a multitude of emotions flooding her head and heart.

"Toni!" Romero approached Toni and embraced her tightly.

David and Red both stood feeling mutual discomfort at the affection unfolding before them. Toni reciprocated the gesture long enough to make sure he was real, then pushed him away gently. Romero just stared into Toni's eyes trying to search her soul. He wanted to be sure she truly forgave him.

"I'm sorry I left the way I did, but . . ." Toni touched his lips with her finger to stop him from continuing.

143

"I don't know where you've been, but I'm so happy you're alright and
I thank you for everything you've done for me." She looked at Red then continued. "But she is the only person you owe and explanation to." Toni told Romero with her heart on fire.

He grabbed her hand and placed it over his heart. "You're never cut off." Romero whispered so only Toni could hear.

She didn't realize until she thought he was dead how she actually felt about Romero. She loved him, and she couldn't deny it to herself, but she would endure the pain of seeing him with another woman if it meant making a family whole.

With as much love as she had for Romero, she was "in love" with David, and she could not deny or jeopardize what she had with him.

But with everything going on in Toni's mind, Red was still stuck on
what Toni said about her donor.

"Toni, I know seeing Romero may be a lot for you right now, but you said something about my blood donor. Who was it?" Red asked.

Toni handed Red the same test results and apology letter she was given by her father. Red silently read the papers in her hands as everyone awaited her reaction. Romero had no idea what was transpiring as he watched the door because the sound of his infant son crying made him more uncomfortable than everything else that was going on.

Red looked up at Toni and a single tear ran down her cheek. It was like everything she had gone through in her life was all making sense. The way her mother and father treated her, the fact that she didn't seem to fit into her house hold in general, not to mention, she looked nothing like Rufus.

She walked around her desk and wrapped her arms around Toni's neck. They hugged and cried until they laughed and reminisced. David and Romero engaged in some male bonding of their own as they shared sports and spiritual views that day.

While bonding with Red, Toni decided that she needed to get Ivey out of finger pointing mode. She thought it was funny that she was the one being the voice of reason in this situation and not her usually more sensible little sister.

"You want to hold your nephew?" Red asked Toni out of the blue.

Toni, without hesitation extended her arms to receive the little handsome bundle of joy. She looked down at her newly found family member and kissed his tiny fingers. She laughed on the inside at the thought that Romero made sure he found a way to become a part of her family.

"I love you nephew." Toni whispered. "And you will be surrounded
with love."

Toni realized an abundance of things that day. First and foremost, she was capable of having emotions that were not taught. And that she was actually more in love with David than she realized. She imagined many times what she would do or how she would feel if she saw Romero again. But her feelings for David withstood Rome's presence.

Toni had formed an inseparable bond with David that was undeniable to them both. It was a bond that even Romero could not only not deny, but he couldn't dispute it; and nor would he try.

# We Meet Again

Quitta hadn't seen Rocky for days when she put two and two together and realized that Rocky was to blame for the disappearance of her diary. Especially after Gwen told her they were scheduled for another meeting with the Principal and Superintendent in reference to some evidence brought to their attention.

"Come here!" Gwen yelled from the living room.

Already knowing where this conversation was going, Quitta reluctantly trudged her way into the room with her mother.

"Ma'am?" She said with the same tone of a person asking, "What the
fuck you want?" And Gwen recognized it.

"Who the hell you talking to like that?" Gwen roared.

"I said ma'am." Quitta said with a diminished attitude.

147

"So what evidence these people got? You gone have me up at this damn school looking crazy cause you lying and shit!" Gwen ranted without a thought as to why her child would tell a lie of this caliber.

Quitta became hot on the inside. She felt like an instant fever had formed under her skin. She couldn't believe with all the things she did to get the attention of her mother, that Gwen was still only worried about herself.

"What difference does it make?" Quitta said barely audible.

"Whatchu say?" Gwen asked in a threatening tone.

"I said, what difference does it make? Once it's over, I'm the one that
gotta see these people every day, not you. But you act like don't nothing or nobody matter but you. All you care about is how this is gone make you look. Have you even thought about how you look already?" Quitta had never verbally disrespected her mother before.

Gwen couldn't believe what Quitta said to her or the tone she spoke to her in. She became infuriated and slapped Quitta with all her might. Quitta grabbed her face in surprise. But to Gwen's surprise, Quitta had slapped her right back before she even realized it.

"Are you fucking crazy!?" Gwen yelled before she grabbed Quitta by the hair and commenced a full out attack.

Before Quitta realized she wasn't mad enough to fight her mother, she

148

was already in the middle of a full-fledged beat down. All she could do was block the blows she could to avoid black eyes and busted lips.

Gwen swung until she was tired and fell back on the sofa. As she sweated and tried to catch her breath, she saw that Quitta's red swollen face was full of tears and pain. Without a word, Quitta got off the floor and walked out the front door.

"Quitta! Where are you going? Get yo ass back here, you know we got a meeting!" Gwen screamed even long after Quitta was out of her sight. "Fuck!" She said throwing a coaster at the screen door.

Gwen had no time to deal with Quitta's outburst. She was on a time schedule and had to be at the school in forty-five minutes. She got dressed and waited as long as she could for Quitta to come to her senses. Deciding to call Quitta's phone sounded like a good idea until she heard it ring from the bedroom.

"Damn." She said as she hung up.

Not knowing what to expect made Gwen apprehensive about the meeting. And somehow, Quitta's absence made her even more uncomfortable. Plus, being the last to arrive and having all eyes on her upon her entrance, made her discomfort apparent.

"Sorry I'm late." Gwen told Ivey, Mr. Farlin, and Mrs. Jarvis.

"No problem Mrs. Benton, have a seat please." Mr. Farlin motioned for her to sit at a table that contained a familiar pink notebook with rainbow writing.

"This was brought to our attention." Mrs. Jarvis said as she pointed to the notebook.

Gwen immediately recognized Quitta's handwriting.

"How did you get this?" Gwen asked.

"We received it anonymously ma'am, but we thought you would be
more interested in the content, than where it came from." Mrs. Jarvis said.

Ivey sat quietly behind her desk watching things play out like a scene in a movie. She watched as Gwen's facial expression changed with every horrifying entry she read in her sixteen-year-old daughter's diary. There was everything from the underlying hate she harbored for both of her parents, to the various sexual conquests she had plotted. The horror etched across Gwen's face was an indication that she had no idea what she was dealing with.

"Mrs. Benton, we feel that you and your daughter are in need of some extensive counseling, and we are more than willing to assist you with that." Mr. Farlin told her.

"Okay." Was all Gwen could say.

With all of her education and career accolades, Gwen felt like a failure for the second time in her life. The first was when she lost her husband to her ego, and now this.

Now Quitta's feelings and the things she said to Gwen that day made
sense. According to the diary, Quitta felt like no one's child. And Gwen

knew she was more than responsible for the way Quitta felt about herself,
Gwen, and her life in general. A mirror had been turned on their life and something had to change.

Agonizing Ecstasy

Vodka couldn't calm Gwen's nerves after the police refused to take a missing person's report for Quitta after only twelve hours. It was after midnight when she finally fell into a tipsy slumber; it was actually the only rest she had gotten since the fiasco with Clarence.

Her cell phone jolted her from her sleep. She didn't recognize the number of the incoming call, but she decided she should answer, considering the circumstances.

"Hello." Gwen said in a groggy tone.

What sounded like a Middle Eastern man replied.

"May I please speak with Gwendolyn Benton?" He asked.

"Yes, how can I help you?"

"Are you the mother of LaQuitta Benton?" He asked with an accent
so heavy, she could barely make out what he said.

"Yes, yes I'm her mother." She said with hopefulness.

"Ma'am, I am Dr. Salib from Saint Louis University Hospital. We found her student identification and pulled her records. From that, I found your information." He informed her.

Gwen couldn't understand why a man with an accent so heavy, would use words with so many syllables. It was aggravating her to have to listen so hard.

"Ma'am, she is in I.C.U. It appears she tried to commit suicide." Gwen couldn't believe what she was hearing. She was prepared to talk to Quitta about the things in her diary in an attempt to repair their relationship.

But now, she was afraid she wouldn't get the chance. She recorded all the information from the doctor she needed, and rushed to the hospital.

When she arrived, Quitta was heavily sedated with tubes in her nose. Gwen stumbled back at the initial sight of her child. She covered her mouth to hold in her cries. The doctor stood close by and waited until she was able to contain her composure.

"What happened?" She finally said.

"From what the report said, she was found in a motel unconscious. But we pumped what appeared to be the equivalent of about twenty ecstasy pills from her stomach. And we also found marijuana and alcohol in her system." Dr. Salib informed her.

"Is she going to be alright?" That was ultimately the only thing Gwen wanted to know.

"It appears that we have been able to rid her system of the toxins and we plan to wake her in a few hours." He told her as if he was getting permission. "It is hopeful." He concluded.

Gwen sat for hours awaiting the chance to see Quitta awake. She even tried to call Quitta's father Franklin, but there was no answer. So, she left him an extensive message detailing everything that had transpired, hoping he would respond for Quitta's sake. She understood the reason for his absence even if Quitta didn't, but now she needed him to be a father.

Today was the first time she was at least honest with herself about the role she played in the demise of her marriage.

As she sat and looked at her daughter, Gwen thought back to a time when they were all a family. But she couldn't think about that without thinking about the way she degraded Franklin for not making as much money as she wanted him to. And then ultimately the restraining order he had to get against her for stalking him after their divorce.

Gwen dozed off momentarily and was awakened by a nurse asking if
Quitta could receive more visitors.

"Who is it?" She was confused because she hadn't talked to anyone.

154

"Mr. Franklin Benton." The nurse said.

Gwen couldn't believe her ears, and she allowed him permission back to see Quitta. She straightened her hair and clothes and prepared to greet him.

He entered the room looking as handsome as ever. Franklin had always been physically Gwen's type. He was six-foot-tall, light complexion, and physically fit. Being a personal trainer by profession made that a given.

As he entered, Gwen was so caught up in the fact that he showed up, that she hadn't noticed his wife, Sheila, walk in behind him, hand in hand. Gwen had to remember why she was there to stop herself from reacting inappropriately. Gwen got control of her composure.

"I'm glad you could come." Gwen addressed Franklin with a handshake.

"What happened?" Sheila asked while she bounced into the room.

"Bitch, don't talk to me!" This time Gwen said unable to contain her anger.

Franklin quickly stood between the two women to diffuse the situation. He was actually regretting showing up.

"What happened?" He asked Gwen, making her answer the question anyway.

Gwen explained everything that the doctors told her to Franklin. He agreed to let her go home to freshen up and get some things for Quitta. She left hurriedly so she could return as soon as possible.

When Gwen arrived home, she noticed her front door was slightly ajar. She looked around to see if she recognized any of the vehicles on her street. All she saw was an old black Cadillac across the street and three other cars she recognized.

Gwen figured with all the excitement, she left the door open while rushing out to go to the hospital. She walked inside and locked the door behind her. Only she didn't realize she was locking herself on the wrong side of the door. She looked in horror as Clarence sat on her couch with her remote in his hand.

"What's up baby? Come over here." He patted the seat on the couch next to him. "Sit yo mutha fuckin ass down!"

Promise


It was eight in the morning and Rocky figured it was the perfect time to get the things she left from Quitta's. She knew Gwen would have already left for work and Quitta was supposed to be at school an hour ago.

She sneaked into the basement the way Quitta had taught her and hoped there had been no barriers put up to stop her from entering. Rocky had strategically placed the belongings she couldn't carry around the basement, so she could come back to get them later, unnoticed.

As she packed her duffle bag, Rocky couldn't help but to recognized what sounded like a struggle taking place upstairs. Rocky was hardly in the mood for a family affair, so she continued to pack and ignored the ruckus she heard. It wasn't until she heard a pleading voice say, "Why are you doing this?" that she decided to sneak upstairs to see what was going on.

Rocky crept through the kitchen quietly and peeked in to the living room to see Gwen sitting on the couch. Rocky noticed the terror in her eyes as she wondered who Gwen was so afraid of.

"Why won't you just leave me alone?" Gwen pleaded.

"Cuz I see how much you like to suck dick, you finna make me some money. I could tell you was a champion." He told her. "So, if you wanna live in peace, I got some work for you." He said making her an offer she'd better not refuse.

"Fuck you nigga, I ain't no fucking prostitute!" Gwen was absolutely offended.

"When I said you belonged to me, I meant it. Do you think all that shit I gave you was for free? Bitch that was an investment, and if you ain't workin'; then you owe me. You think you can afford to pay me back for all the shit I gave you?" Clarence said revealing his pimp occupation.

As Rocky crept through the dining room area, she noticed that Gwen's
capturer only had a Swiss blade. But when she got closer she realized she was face-to-face with the devil himself, and she knew she had a promise to keep.

Rocky quickly and quietly stepped into the living room aiming her chrome, snub nosed 357 Magnum, directly at Smiley, her mother's murderer.

"Baby girl, whatchu think you doin' with that?" He laughed heartily like he had been told a joke. "This is perfect, I get two for one." He said with enough pride and arrogance for ten men.

Then he looked over and realized that Rocky was still aiming her gun directly at his head.

"Mrs. Benton, call the police." Rocky instructed.

"Little lady, give me that gun before you hurt yourself." Clarence,
a.k.a. Smiley said walking up to Rocky to take possession of her weapon.

"If yo slimey ass takes one more step, I promise it'll be your last." Rocky tried to warn him.

Clarence decided to call her bluff. He tilted his head to the left and proceeded to take one more step. But to his demise, Rocky wasn't bluffing. Before his foot could touch the ground, he was already on his back. When he attempted to lift his head, all he could see was a smoking hole in his own chest before he lost consciousness and took his last breath.

Rocky lowered the smoking gun to see Gwen's mascara smeared, tear covered face. She held her cell phone in one hand and the police were within seconds from the house.

"Thank you." Was all Gwen could say to Rocky before she was carried away in cuffs.

"I couldn't break my promise." Rocky said right before they pushed
her head down into the back seat of the police car.

Gwen wouldn't wish death on anyone, but as long as Clarence was out of her life for good, she was comfortable with the maniac's demise. Her only regret was that she didn't get a chance to tell Rocky about Quitta's condition. Whatever reservations Gwen had about Rocky before today, were all gone.

And what she learned from the entire incident was never to judge a book by its cover.

In Due "Time"


Ivey had yet to speak with Randy or tell anyone other than Brandon that she was pregnant. She was moody and sick, but Brandon delicately handled her while he struggled not to tell anyone about his baby, at Ivey's request.

Ivey also made sure that Quitta, Gwen, and Franklin got the counseling they needed. Quitta was apologetic about the events and had even forgiven Rocky for stealing her diary. She was also very grateful to Rocky for saving her mother's life.

Rocky however, although satisfied that she was rid of the monster that murdered her mother, was missing her little sisters immensely. Before she shot and killed the man she knew as Smiley, she still picked up Laniah and Mariah from school every day like clockwork. They promised not to tell Mama Isa, and they would depart from one another a block away from their house.

Now she was faced with gun charges at age sixteen. She wasn't charged with murder because between her and Gwen's statements, it was clear self-defense. And since leaving Quitta's she had lived on the street, or to and from whatever ex-girlfriend's house she could. So, for the first day or so, Rocky was actually relieved to have a steady roof over her head and food to eat. It wasn't until she realized that she was faced with being charged as an adult and five years in prison that Rocky knew she needed help. The business card she received from Ivey the day she left school came to mind as she was faced with losing five years of her life.

It was Sunday afternoon and Ivey sat behind the desk in her office at home trying not to throw-up while she organized her files. She remembered her mother Lois telling friends to use ginger as a remedy for morning sickness when she was young. She sat drinking Ginger Tea and eating Ginger Snaps when an unfamiliar phone number came across her cell phone.

"Ivey Cameron." She said in her best professional tone.

"You have a collect call from, 'Mrs. Cameron this is Rocky. I put you on my list, please come visit tomorrow morning at ten. I need your help.' Will you accept the charges?"

Ivey tried to comprehend the words that originally sound like gibberish until she put them all together.

The next day, Ivey took a few hours off work to go to the Juvenile Center to visit Rocky. After going through security checks, she was finally admitted into the visiting room to see Rocky.

The room was filled with teenagers and parents or guardians, talking to and crying with their children. Ivey approached the table and sat across from Rocky. She looked into her eyes and saw the pain, fear, and confusion that filled them.

"Thank you for coming to see me Mrs. Cameron." Rocky said humbly.

Ivey reached across the table and grabbed her hands.

"I'm glad you called. Are you alright?" Ivey asked with concern for the young girl in such a cruel place.

"I don't know, this seems to be the most stability I have, being homeless and all. But even worse, they're trying to get me on 1$^{st}$ degree murder and a gun charge. I could be facing twenty years to life!" Rocky's hope seemed to descend to the floor with her eyes.

"Look at me." Ivey demanded. "You have to believe this situation will work out for the best, beyond a shadow of a doubt. I'm going to do everything I can to help you." Ivey promised.

"I need one more favor." Rocky said hoping she wasn't asking too much.

"Anything."

"Can you check on my little sisters Laniah and Mariah for me? We
don't have our mother or a father, all we have is each other. I have to know they're okay and they need to know why I haven't been to see them. I want them to know that I have not and would never abandon them. I know they're worried." Rocky said with tears in her eyes and wisdom beyond her years.

The situation in Ivey's own life played in her head like a drive-in movie. She recognized not only the wisdom in this young girl's words, but also the father and family she had taken for granted.

"I promise." Ivey's words sent butterflies through Rocky's stomach.

Rocky went back to her cell with a peace of mind that day. She maintained the Faith that Ivey told her to and she read the Bible and literature Ivey left for her on her visit. And Ivey left with a sense of appreciation for EVERYTHING she had.

## Old Feelings

As Romero looked at himself in the mirror, he couldn't help but to think about seeing Toni. He hadn't lied to Red when he told her he loved her. But he couldn't deny the fact that he was still in love with Toni and he realized it that day, along with the fact that Toni's heart belong to David.

After finding out there was one Brown boy left and after Toni, Romero couldn't deny the feeling that there was still unfinished business. But he also continued to struggle with the thought of jeopardizing his family, again.

Despite his feelings for Toni, he was happy with Red. They got along
and they fit together perfectly, which was sometimes a problem for Romero. He was afraid when things came too easily for him.

Red peeked into the bathroom and stared at Romero's brown chiseled frame from behind, and his reflection in the mirror.

"Earth to Romero." Red teased.

"What's up babe?" He gave her eye contact through the mirror as he
answered.

"I need you to go to the store please. RJ needs pampers and wipes." She smiled as if he had a choice in the matter.

"I'm already gone."


When Romero closed the front door behind him, he noticed the tail end of a blue SUV pulling away from the house. He instantly became suspicious as he walked to his car. He looked around the side of the house and under both cars. His street instincts kicked in when he approached his rental car to open the driver's door. Romero hesitated before getting inside the car.

BOOM!

Red almost jumped out of her skin when she heard the explosion that sounded like it was coming from inside her house. She ran down the stairs to the sight of Romero putting the fire out on the sleeve of his jacket, and he was bleeding from his forehead. He was stunned, but his instincts made him quickly snap into action.

"I've gotta go?" Romero said in a hurry, but Red wouldn't allow it.

"What's going on?" Where are you going?" Red was frantic.

"Call the police. Tell them you were about to leave, and you forgot your purse and went back inside, then you heard an explosion. Have them check the Lexus and the perimeter of the house for anything else." Romero instructed her on auto pilot.

"Where are you going? Please don't leave us again!" Red cried.

He grabbed her face to calm her down; time was of the essence.

"Baby listen to me, I will be back. Do what I said and I'll take care of everything else." He kissed her and looked into her eyes to make sure she was still with him.

He saw the fear of the possibility of never seeing him again and the love she had for him, but she was all there otherwise. And without speaking he left, and Red knew exactly where he was headed.

*Toni's Loft*

Toni heard ramblings in her living room as she finished up her shower. She turned off the water and stood quietly for a few moments. There were voices, male and female coming from outside the bathroom door.
She began to shake nervously when she realized her best means of protection was in her night table drawer. Trying to see if she could recognize any voices, she put her ear to the door and locked it as gently and quietly as possible.

BANG!

"Get out here girl, I got something for you." She clearly recognized the voice, it was David.

Toni gave a sigh of relief as she grabbed her robe and exited the bathroom to see what was going on. When she got to the living room, David stood next to a beautiful Latino woman.

She was shapely and petite, but her ass was almost too big for her small frame. Her long, black, curly hair was almost waist length. After taking her all in, Toni finally addressed David.

"What's this?' Toni asked referring to the Spanish goddess that was seducing Toni with her eyes.

"This is what you want isn't it?" He asked.

"No, I want you." Toni was as confused as ever.

David began to strip out of his clothes and the unidentified vixen followed suit. After seeing David naked, the protest Toni had planned went completely out the window.

He walked over to Toni and removed her robe. She couldn't believe what was happening, but she refused to stop it. David gently rubbed her breast as he planted sweet, soft kisses on her neck and shoulders. He wrapped his arms around her waist and pulled her closer, and then he kissed her unlike he ever had. They always contained their passion, so they wouldn't violate their promise to God. But now, something had definitely changed.

The sexy Spaniard was now behind Toni assisting David with the pleasuring of her. She caressed and sucked everything that wasn't in David's hand or mouth. Toni could hardly contain her screams as they both pleasured her until she climaxed. They were all three still standing in the living room and David's beautiful penis stood with them.

He watched her as her body convulsed and juices ran down the inside of both legs. David kissed her again before turning her around, leaning her over the back of the chair, and penetrating her from behind. Toni gasped as David entered her with his thick nine-inch shaft. Their voluptuous visitor was sure not to be left out as she fondled and licked Toni's nipples. David stroked her long and slow at first, being mindful of how long it had been since her last sexual encounter. But as she began to match his strokes, he quickened his pace and so did she. They both screamed simultaneously as they ejaculated together.

Guilt didn't come over her until her orgasm was over and her head returned to clarity.

"What did we just do?" Toni's eyes showed shame as she looked up at David with a smile on his face.

Suddenly, her chest felt heavy and her body felt like she was being weighed down. It was hard for her to breath and she couldn't understand what was happening to her. As she reached for David, he seemed to get further and further away.

It wasn't until she began to struggle with an unidentified stranger, that she realized it had all been a dream, but not anymore. She was wide awake.

She fought to pull the skull cap from the stranger's head as she took several violent blows to the face. Toni didn't hesitate to return those hits blow for blow. He seemed surprised by her strength as he wrestled with her to gain control.

Toni was in full survival mode and refused to be overtaken. She kept trying to scream, but he would put his hand over her mouth to prevent it. But his last attempt to quiet her would be a fatal one.

169

"Aaaaaaauugh!" He screamed to the top of his lungs as blood gushed from between Toni's teeth.

In one motion, Toni reached in her night table drawer and snatched the skull cap from her assailant's head. Just as she suspected it was Troy Brown. Flashes of her rape surfaced as she pointed the gun in his direction. They both were out of breath from the struggle, but Troy saw rage in Toni's eyes.

"Whatchu gone do bitch, kill me? I'm already dead!" He charged, knocking the gun across the room and Toni onto her back.

Now on the floor, Toni fought to get Troy off of her. She punched and
scratched at his face in an effort to overcome him. But before she could get the best of him, Troy punched Toni in the face with all his might. She was knocked unconscious long enough for him to get his hands firmly around her neck.

Troy began to squeeze as he watched Toni's eyes open as wide as they could, while she gasped for air. She clawed at his face and got nothing but a tighter grasp around her throat as a response. Toni started to slip in and out of consciousness and she was sure this was the end.

She saw the shadow of what looked like an angel and started to succumb to the urge to let go of this life. Then suddenly, she was able to breath. When she came into full consciousness, she realized the angel was Romero, once again. He stood in the doorway of her apartment holding the gun he bought her a few years before, pointing it directly at Troy.

It was a true standoff. They watched each other intensely for the other's next move. Without warning, Troy pulled a knife from his back and lifted it over Toni's barely conscious body.

POW! POW! POW!

Three bullets ripped through Troy's chest causing him to drop the knife and collapse backward onto the floor.

Toni struggled to get up and staggered in Romero's direction as he met her half way and caught her in his arms. He looked her over to be sure she was okay. He noticed a black eye starting to form and bruising around her neck.

"Are you okay?" Romero asked rubbing his hand gently down the side of her face.

Toni couldn't answer; she just broke down into tears. She cried out loud and buried her face in his chest.

"My job is done. Now I can hand you over to him with a clear
conscious." Romero said before he kissed her on the forehead and left.

Toni knew the routine and Rome knew she needed no instruction.
She wiped his prints off the gun and replaced them with hers. She picked up the phone and dialed 911.

"Operator, I just killed an intruder."

# The Invite

Toni and David's wedding had been pushed back a month due to the violent struggle she had with Troy Brown. But at this point, she was just happy to have David and to be alive at all. It had been a week since the incident and she hadn't heard anything from Red or Romero. Toni saw the explosion in Chesterfield on the news, but was cautious not to arouse suspicion with the police by contacting either of them right now.

She felt completely safe for the first time in a long while. Being at home alone was no longer a scary feeling as she sifted through her mail barefoot and half naked. She did a double take when she saw an envelope from Ivey. When she opened it, there was a formal invite to dinner at Ivey's house. She wondered why she hadn't just called, when Toni noticed a note that said, "Attendance is required for ALL PARTIES, NO EXCEPTIONS." Then she realized she wasn't the only person invited. The dinner was that coming Sunday at four p.m. sharp.

*Sunday Evening*

Toni arrived an hour early just in case Ivey needed help with any last-minute details. When she approached the door, Ivey had it opened before Toni could even knock.

"Oh, you're early. Would you like something to drink?" Ivey asked sounding like an official hostess.

"Um, well I actually carne to see if you needed any help." Toni offered.

"No ma'am, I have everything under control thank you."

"Well then, I'll take a glass of red wine if you have any." Toni requested.

Ivey poured Toni a glass of the Pinot Noir that she swore never to touch again, and escorted her to the family room.

"Let me know if you need anything. Make yourself at home." Ivey
said before disappearing back into the kitchen.

Toni listened to the slow, soft jazz playing as she sipped her glass of wine. The aroma of dinner was like an air freshener all over the house, but the room felt more like a waiting area as she sat alone waiting for what was to come next.
The door opened and Ivey escorted David inside. Toni stood to greet him.

"Hey baby, do you know what this is about?" He asked Toni in the
midst of their kisses.

"Nope not yet, I'm just as clueless as you are. She won't even let me help with anything." Toni told David.

174

"Can I ask you something?" She asked David seriously.

"Anything." He replied.

"How can you still love me after all that's happened?" Toni asked, almost afraid of the answer.

"Baby, everything we go through makes me realize I would lose my mind without you. You're my colorful view, remember? And now that I've seen that view, I can't live without it." David had never been sincerer with anyone in his life.

He loved Toni for everything she was and all he knew she would become. No matter how much they had gone through, David knew she was sent to him from God. Some may have seen it the other way around, but David knew better.

"I don't deserve you." Toni said as she laid her head on David's
chest.

They embraced for a few minutes and then the door opened again.
This time Regina and Randy entered delighted to see them.

Randy had only seen Toni once since the tragedy and was happy to see that she was doing so well. Toni was agitated by the over-protective behavior of her father, so she banned him from her apartment for a few days.

"I see you're doing better." Randy observed.

"Yes daddy, I managed to get better without you fluffing my pillow and putting socks on my feet." Toni said joking but serious.

"Give him a break baby; he's just being a dad." David said coming to
Randy's defense.

The family room was getting full by the minute, so when the door opened a third time, everyone seemed surprised. The few silent seconds had everyone full of anticipation. Then to everyone's surprise, Red appeared in the doorway. Toni wanted so badly to ask about Romero, but she didn't want to make things anymore awkward than they already were.

Then as if her mind was being read, Romero appeared in the doorway behind Red, holding RJ in his arms. Toni walked up to Red and gave her a hug, to initiate her welcome. And David gave Romero a long, firm gratuitous handshake.

Red and Toni released their embrace and Red walked directly up to Randy. She looked at the features in his face and for the first time she could see where she came from. She put her arms around Randy's neck and began to cry silently. Randy wrapped his arms around his daughter for the first time and felt an instant connection.

"Thank you." She whispered. "No, thank you." He replied.

*Dinner*

After all of Ivey's dinner guests arrived, she escorted them all to the dining room. Brandon assisted her with strategically placing everyone where she wanted them to be seated at the table. Everyone noticed an empty seat, but decided they would wait to see what the rest of the evening held, Ivey seemed to be full of surprises.

"I would like to thank everyone for coming this evening. I have a few
announcements to make as well as a few apologies. First and foremost, I want to say thank you to my husband for not only loving me, but tolerating me these past few weeks. I know it hasn't been easy." She said smiling at Brandon and blowing a kiss in his direction.

"Dad, I want to apologize to you for the way I reacted and the things I said to you. I will never disrespect you that way again. Please forgive me." Ivey pleaded with Randy.

"Of course, I forgive you baby girl." Randy replied.

"Red, I have to apologize to you as well for not reaching out to you sooner. You didn't ask for any of this and it wasn't fair for me to treat you like it was your fault. So from this day forward, you have a sister in me." Ivey said sincerely. "Just don't forget, I'm still the youngest." She joked as she continued.

Ivey smiled and nodded her head in acceptance as she rocked RJ on her shoulder.

"Now moving on to the announcements. First, Toni our grant proposal went through and we are now the CEOs of our own non-profit organization!" Ivey handed Toni the envelope containing the final paperwork as she spoke.

Toni stood to hug Ivey as the family applauded with pride.

"Okay, let me keep this party going. Secondly, and the reason for my recent behavior." She paused. "I'm pregnant!"

Oohs and aahs were exchanged as everyone hugged and kissed and congratulated the newlyweds turn parents.

"And finally, I would like to welcome someone into our loving but dysfunctional family. We will have a guest staying here with us for a little while. Come on out sweetheart!" Ivey yelled toward the spare bedroom. "I would like everyone to meet and welcome Raquel Santiago."

Life's Revival
(six months later)


This year's annual church revival was to recognize the Pastor's 25th Anniversary. The event had been a big deal for the church and was advertised all over the community.

Toni had been Mrs. David James for five months now and she was more in love than she ever thought possible. So, she felt great pride when she saw her husband on the pulpit. They had been through hell and high water, but their happiness only reflected that they shared nothing but joyous times.

Ivey and Brandon sat on the front bench as usual. Brandon sat next to Ivey with a constant hand on her belly. He felt if she was close enough for him to touch her, he wouldn't miss a kick, a punch, or a roll. As irritating as it was to Ivey, she still thought it was cute that he was so excited about the baby. He waited on her hand and foot, and even suggested that she go out on maternity leave early on a few occasions.

Rocky had now become a permanent fixture at the church and was a junior mentor for the youth program. Since going to live with Ivey, she had tried to rebuild the missing pieces of her life. She was forever grateful to Ivey when she showed up in court with an attorney to represent her case. The Judge heard the circumstances and gave her two years' probation. She was remanded into Ivey's custody and Ivey saw to it that she got visitation with her sisters. Seven months ago, she was living a nightmare. Now she had a foundation, a peace of mind, and a future, thanks to Ivey. Their relationship had formed an irreversible bond between them and Rocky had become family, like the little sister she never had.

The program was about to start when Ivey nudged Toni and nodded her head in the direction of Romero, Red, and family. They waved from across the church and Ivey continued to survey the audience. As she admired the turnout, she was completely astonished when she noticed Mama Isa walk in with the twins. This time Ivey made eye contact with Rocky.

They both looked in the direction of the entrance when Rocky's entire being lit up at the sight of her little sisters. She quickly made her way through the crowd to greet them. Ivey watched as the girls fought for Rocky's hugs and kisses.

Mama Isa observed the love the three sisters had for one another. She realized that keeping Laniah and Mariah away from their sister, would not only cause them even more emotional turmoil, but it would also cause them to harbor resentment against her. She had already lost a daughter to her judgment and selfishness; she refused to destroy the only family she had left.

Rocky found a seat with her family when she felt a light tap on her shoulder. When she turned, she was surprised to see Gwen and Quitta.

"Hello Raquel." Gwen greeted her first.

"What's up Rocky?" Quitta said giving her friend a hug.

"Hi. I'm glad y'all came out." Rocky said surprised to see them at
all.

The past few months proved to be promising for Rocky and Quitta's friendship. Quitta was no longer starved for the inappropriate attention of men, so it allowed Rocky to find out who the real Quitta was, and she liked her much more than old Quitta.

Gwen was so grateful to Rocky for risking her own life to save hers, that even if Quitta and Rocky had not continued on as friends, she would have been a permanent part of her life anyway. Gwen would do anything for Rocky.

"Mrs. Cameron called and told me about the revival. Where is she?" Gwen asked.

"Down front where she always is." Rocky said pointing to the front of the church.

She grabbed Quitta's hand and hightailed it to the front row.

"Hello Mrs. Cameron. Thank you for inviting us." Gwen said.

"Thank you for coming. Hello LaQuitta. How are you?" Ivey asked.

"I'm great actually! But I need to do something." Quitta said looking
in Brandon's direction.

Seeing Ivey and Rocky at school made it easy for Quitta to apologize to them and make whatever amends she needed to. Brandon was well aware of Quitta's position, but she was taught in therapy to apologize to those she had wronged. And she felt she had done the most damage to him.

"May I?" Quitta asked Ivey nodding in Brandon's direction.

Ivey stepped to the side to allow Quitta access to him.

"Excuse me, can I please talk to you for a minute?" Quitta asked Brandon.

"Of course. What can I do for you?" He acted as if the sight of her didn't cause him anxiety.

"Well, I just want to apologize directly to you. I've told Mrs. Cameron how sorry I am, but I feel you deserve to hear it from me. I wasn't thinking about anything but myself. I was hurt, so I hurt other people. I just hope you can find it in your heart to forgive me." Quitta said with sincerity.

"Thank you. It's a real honorable thing for you to do. And of course, I forgive you." Brandon extended his arms for an appropriate embrace.

Ivey happily witnessed the exchange. She had seen the change in Quitta since her father re-entered her life and knew she had unlimited potential.

The congregation began to wind down for the opening of the service. David in all his handsome glory had everyone's attention, especially Toni's. She felt the way she did the first time she laid eyes on him at the very same pulpit. Her attraction for him was like a burning fire, but her love for him surpassed any emotion she had ever experienced.

Toni looked across the church at Romero and his new family. She knew she could never love him the way he wanted her to, but Red did, and they seemed happy with each other.

"Let the church say Amen!" David's voice blasted through the speakers.

"Amen!" The congregation sang in unison.

"I would first like to commemorate Pastor Cameron on his 25th church anniversary celebration! Amen!" David welcomed the church's applause on the Pastor's behalf.

"Today church, I would like to focus on God's mercy and forgiveness. I remember as a child, I would fight with one of the kids then we would make up. But that foundation is now set. Now that we've fought, we tolerate each other because we still have friends in common. But the truth is, we are now waiting for any opportunity to fight again. That's because of a lack of true forgiveness and mercy.

Even as adults we seem to live by the human concept, 'I forgive you,
but I won't forget.' And I say human concept because the spirit forgives and forgets. God would not promise to wash us clean if he planned to keep a tally of all the wrong he's already forgiven us for. No one is perfect. We were all born in sin and have fallen short of his glory. All He wants from us is to use our free will to acknowledge our sins and ask for his forgiveness and he will show us mercy!

Let's turn to Acts 26:6-31. 6 And now I stand and am judged for the hope of the promise made of God, unto our fathers:

7 Unto which promise our twelve tribes, instantly serving God day and night, hope to come. For which hope's sake, King Agrippa, I am accused of the Jews. 8 Why should it be thought a thing incredible with you, that God should raise the dead?
9 I verily thought with myself, that I ought to do many things contrary to the name of Jesus of Nazareth. 10 Which thing I also did in Jerusalem: and many of the saints did I shut up in prison, having received authority from the chief priests; and when they were put to death, I gave my voice against them. 11 And I punished them oft in every synagogue, and compelled them to blaspheme; and being exceedingly mad against them, I persecuted them even unto strange cities.
12 Whereupon as I went to Damascus with authority and commission from the chief priests, 13 At midday, O king, I saw in the way a light from heaven, above the brightness of the sun, shining round about me and them which journeyed with me. 14 And when we were all fallen to the earth, I heard a voice speaking unto me, and saying in the Hebrew tongue, Saul, Saul, why persecutes! Thou me? It is hard for thee to kick against the pricks. 15 And I said, who art thou, Lord? And he said, I am Jesus whom thou persecutes! 16 But rise, and stand upon thy feet: for I have appeared unto thee for this purpose, to make thee a minister and a witness both of these things which thou hast seen, and of those things in the which I will appear unto thee; 17 Delivering thee from the people, and from the Gentiles, unto whom now I send thee, 18 To open their eyes, and to tum them from darkness to light, and from the power of Satan unto God, that they may receive forgiveness of sins, and inheritance among them which are sanctified by faith that is in me. 19 Whereupon, O king Agrippa, I was not disobedient unto the heavenly vision: 20 But shewed first unto them of Damascus, and at Jerusalem, and

throughout all the coasts of Judaea, and then to the Gentiles, that they should repent and tum to God, and do works meet for repentance. 21 For these causes the Jews caught me in the temple, and went about to kill me.

Now Paul was a persecutor and a murderer of Jews. God not only forgave him and showed him mercy, he also put an anointing over Paul's life. If God can find the mercy to forgive Paul for persecuting his people, then we should be able to forgive and forget.

Matthew 7:1-2 says, Judge not, that ye be not judged. For with what judgment ye judge, ye shall be judged: and with what measure ye mete, it shall be measured to you again.

Sounds like forgive and forget to me. Otherwise, be judged with the
same resentment and unforgiving heart."

David's sermon that day hit home for a lot of people. He managed to touch the hearts of at least twenty people that came up to join the church that day. The choir also uplifted the church with spirit filled selections.

As services were coming to an end, Ivey and Toni stood in front of the church to make the church announcements.

"Amen church! I pray everyone has enjoyed the fellowship this evening." Ivey began.

"Amen!" The congregation responded.

"First, I would like to announce the ground breaking of our new charity housing complex, The Youth House!" Ivey said excitedly. "But most importantly, our first tenant will be God

Kingdom's own, Raquel Santiago. I just want you to know how proud we all are of your progress and maturity." Ivey said provoking applause.

Then David reached down to hand Toni an additional note. Toni elbowed Ivey and handed her the paper. They both looked at one another with surprise and continued.

"And last but definitely not least, we would like to congratulate our sister Drea Mason and our soon to be brother-in-law Romero Wallace on their recent engagement! Amen!" Ivey announced.

Toni's initial reaction started in the pit of her stomach. She didn't know whether to identify it as surprise or jealousy. But by the time the feeling reached her heart, all she could feel was David. And that was the only feeling that mattered. She realized now that she had truly made the right decision in her life.

Me and Mrs. James


After their wedding, Toni broke the lease on her apartment and moved in with David. They discussed moving into a place of their own, but Toni was smitten with David's three bedroom one and a half bath colonial style home. Her only concern was whether or not David would allow her to make it her own; which turned out to be no concern at all.

About a month after she was moved in, the house was the perfect combination of Toni and David together. He had no arguments about the decor; he actually loved every aspect of what she had done. Everything was modernized, but she left a hint of nostalgia for David's sake.

The revival that day was uplifting and left a positive energy in both their spirits. It was actually a turn on to Toni every time she saw Deacon David James on the pulpit. She prayed it wasn't a sin, but she couldn't help herself. All she could think was, *all of that belongs to me*. And an instant feeling of euphoria would come over her.

So tonight, they had only been home about ten minutes before Toni slipped into nothing and began to seduce her husband. He already knew the routine when she entered the dining room wearing nothing but a chocolate colored thong.

"What are you up to Mrs. James?" David asked rhetorically.

She didn't say a word. Toni slowly unbuttoned David's shirt, kissing his chest with each open button. David moaned with pleasure and his loins began to react. By the time she made it to his pants, his love muscle was fighting to be free. Toni released the beast and continued to undress David while he leaned against the Cherry wood dining room table.

Even though Toni was now saved, she was still hood and was determined to keep the excitement in her marriage. She connected her iPhone to the stereo and had Meek Mills *It's Me,* cued up to play. As soon as David was in all his birthday suit glory, she pushed play.

"Ass so fat I need a lap dance." Blared through the speakers and Toni proceeded to give David the raunchiest lap dance he had ever seen, let alone experienced.

As she danced she put on her best video girl moves. All David could think was that he never, in a million years, thought he would have a wife so sexy. He rubbed and caressed the parts of her he could get his hands on while she gyrated.

The lap dance quickly turned into a sexcapade as Toni began to grind on his manhood. Her thong was no match for the nine-inch erection he toted. As she continued to grind, his penis penetrated her wetness. She gasped a breath of pleasure as he filled her up. They made love on every inch of the dining room table until she was sore, and he had no more energy to offer. Needless to say, they more than made up for lost time.

188

"It should be a sin for sex to be this good." Toni said trying to catch her breath.

"Well technically . . ."

"Shut up Deacon." Toni said interrupting the sermon to follow.

David laughed and then looked up at the goddess straddling his lap.

"Why didn't you make the announcement today?" He asked.

"Because, it was already a lot to absorb today. I have time to tell them. Why didn't you make the announcement?" Toni threw back at him.

"I'm following your lead on this baby. Plus, I don't know if I'm ready for the reaction." He admitted.

"I totally understand. I think I've had enough attention to last a life
time." Toni said.

"Me too." David said kissing the miniature bump in her stomach. "I
love you Mrs. James." He told her with that love in his eyes.

Toni rubbed her belly and kissed his forehead.

"We love you too, daddy."

## Q&A

1. Who are your favorite characters? Why?

2. What character do you see yourself as? Why?

3. Did you realize Clarence and Smiley was the same person? If so, when?

4. Give LaQuitta your own psychological evaluation?

5. Is Toni and Romero's relationship really over?

6. Which characters do you like the least? Why?

7. How do you feel about Brenda as a woman, wife, and mother?

8. What was the message(s) in the book?

Made in the USA
Monee, IL
04 December 2021

83835200R10105